BLOOD LOSS

The Collector #2

MATHIAS G. B. COLWELL

BLOOD LOSS, THE COLLECTOR #3
Copyright © 2015-2017 by Mathias G. B. Colwell

ISBN: 978-1-68046-196-1

First Printing: 2015

Melange Books, LLC
White Bear Lake, MN 55110
www.melange-books.com

Published in the United States of America.

Cover Design by Ashley Redbird Designs

UNTITLED

Published by
Melange Books, LLC
White Bear Lake, MN 55110
www.melange-books.com

ISBN: 978-1-68046-197-8

Published in the United States of America.

Cover Design by Stephanie Flint

For Jon.
Thank you for the many hours spent indulging in our mutual delight of all things
fantastical.

CHAPTER ONE

Philip poked his head inside the cave and peered into the gloom, trying to catch a glimpse of what lay within this hole in the mountain. Unfortunately, keen vision in the dark wasn't on the list of exceptional abilities that his genetic makeup afforded him.

A howling growl rumbled through the darkness of the cave and *Philip's skin prickled, not from the crisp mountain air, but from the* sinister sound of his foe becoming aware of an intruder. It must have smelled him! Trolls had a strong sense of smell, much like many wild creatures, and they certainly seemed closer to beasts than humans. One of the reasons he'd had such difficulty accepting his own trollish roots. After all, what kind of man was part beast—part troll?

Philip crouched, listening to the lumbering steps of the troll making its way from the dark recesses within. His quarry was a high functioning predator, one he'd trailed to its lair, a rocky cave high in the mountains of Norway.

The sound of crunching reached his ears. It had to be old bones snapping beneath the weight of the troll's feet as it moved closer and a dark silhouette appeared.

Still in a crouch, Philip warily backed away from the mouth of the cave, waiting for the monster to emerge. Just because he'd trailed the creature here—actions that would be thought foolhardy by most—didn't mean Philip didn't plan to be careful. Giving yourself room to maneuver

1

around a troll was vital. A smile twisted his lips as paradoxically he realized if he died up here in the high passes without Alayna by his side, she'd kill him herself.

His smile faded. Today, pitting himself against what was likely to be an angry and disturbed troll might yield just the outcome Alayna so feared—his death.

The troll emerged fully from the darkness of the cave with a final lurch. For a brief instant uncertainty flooded Philip. The creature was likely ten feet tall if it stood up straight! But instead, it swung its powerful body out of the cave on all fours, not unlike the great apes of the south. Hunched shoulders bulged with muscle, making the creature much quicker than it looked at first glance.

Not for the first time, Philip was amazed that somehow his parents had managed to subdue a troll long enough to obtain a vial of its blood in order to heal him. Just the two of them, and they had been only human. It was a testimony of the power of love that could drive a mother and father to protect their child. The infusion of troll blood was also the reason Philip experienced increased strength and health, as well as imperviousness to some forms of magic.

A brutish face twisted up in a menacing growl, as the troll emitted a gurgling groan of anger. Philip winced at imaging the bits of meat, bone, or gristle, which might be caught in its throat to give the beast's growl that wet, burbling sound. A scattered array of sharp and blunt, mismatching teeth rowed its powerful jaws, jaws that could snap small trees and would make quick work of human bone.

Again, a wash of nerves flooded Philip. Once upon a time his nerves had been a familiar sensation, creating a pit in his stomach just before a fight, letting him know he wanted to live, wanted to survive, and was terrified. He'd felt it every time on a collection run for the Collectors Guild, fighting everything from werewolves to vampires, witches and fauns.

In his many years as a Guild member, he'd had access to all manner of tricks and weapons in order to tip the balance of the fight in his favor. Silver to counteract werewolves, stakes to fight vampires, and the list continued. But here in front of this beast it was just him, his fists, and whatever supernatural abilities he could tap. Suddenly, following the troll to its lair didn't seem like such a good idea.

When Philip had been a Collector, pretending to be fully human, he'd never sought out a conflict unnecessarily, and yet here he was, of his own volition, about to singlehandedly fight the biggest mountain troll he had ever seen.

What had driven him to this place, at this time? Why had he abandoned Alayna, slipping away in the dark of pre-morning as she slumbered by the coals of their fire, still full of a meal of stag from last night.

I should run, Philip thought, tightening his muscles to spring into flight, just as the troll swung a gigantic, boulder-sized fist at him.

Instinctively Philip ducked into a roll to avoid the blow and came to his feet a little to his left. He always kept his tunic unlaced at the neck and had ripped off the sleeves, granting him freedom of movement, a vital skill now that he lived off the land and no longer bowed to the conventions of society.

Blood rushed to Philip's head as the troll's blow landed on the ground to his right, creating a divot the size of a small boulder. Suddenly, exhilaration replaced fear, anticipation replaced caution, and the wild part of himself broke free, the non-human part that relished a fight, and seemed to be growing stronger and stronger each day.

Philip grinned viciously, realizing why he was here—the test of arms, skill and tenacity that lay before him. The troll swung another massive fist, and this time Philip couldn't avoid the punch completely and he recoiled from the glancing blow, which sent, him sailing into a boulder a few feet to the side.

The force of the blow would have crumpled a man, but Philip was not just a man. The troll blood infused during his youth granted him strength, and healing abilities. He leaped back up, wiping blood from his mouth.

The troll advanced again, growling. At the low rumble, all caution left Philip and he threw back his head and howled as much as a human's vocal chords would allow, releasing pent up energy and elation at the prospect of battle. Then he charged at the troll.

Closing the distance in a few steps, he began pummeling the creature's thickly fatted gut. His maneuver had placed him inside the reach of the beast's large and dangerous arms. After several of the creature's futile attempts to swat him, Philip directed a blow at the creature's knee, his inhuman strength delivering a much more powerful blow than the beast expected.

The troll crumpled to one side under its weight and the pain of the injured knee, but also managed to swat at Philip again, this time with an open hand. This blow once more sent Philip head over heels, crashing into a tree and falling to the hard packed earth.

The impact stunned Philip and he shook his head to clear the fog of pain from his mind. The troll lumbered to its feet a bit more slowly, favoring its pained leg. They circled each other again, this time both more cautious in their movements.

An exultant surge of adrenalin and raw joy pulsated inside Philip. For the first time since reaching the cave, he unleashed the wilderness within him, letting it radiate out in waves of wild anger and killing lust. Yielding to your instincts—your nature—provided an addictive release difficult to describe but impossible to live without once you'd experienced it.

Philip closed the distance between him and his foe at a quick run, thinking to attack the wounded knee again and render the troll unable to support its own weight. However, he'd drastically underestimated the speed of the monster. As he was running forwards, the beast whipped one of its stony hands around and snatched him up the way a man might grasp an unruly puppy looking to try its fangs on the master.

The troll shook him until he could barely tell which way was up. Philip tried to peel the fingers of the troll from around his waist, but to no avail, only managing to slice open his palm on one of its sharper nails. The blood flowed freely from Philip's hand and the scent of the hot, red liquid triggered a natural and predatory reflex for the troll to eat.

Raising Philip towards its mouth, the troll opened its jaws to take a huge bite. Desperately, Philip leveraged his body upwards, enough to free his arms. As he approached the gaping maw, he swung as hard as he could and his fist, callused from years of brawling, crashed into the creature's mouth, sending a spray of teeth and knocking the troll backwards.

It dropped him from the height of a few feet and he landed painfully. Although unsteady on his feet, Philip knew he had to press his advantage. The troll seemed uncharacteristically dazed from the blow but was still licking some of Philip's blood from its hand with a leathery tongue. He knew he'd only have a few moments before the creature's natural healing abilities took effect. He had to act now, and fast.

Philip grabbed a stone and darted in close, smashing the rock against the side of the troll's head. The rock shattered with the powerful blow but it achieved Philip's goal of knocking the troll unconscious.

Backing away, Philip wasn't sure if it was really out cold or just stunned. He could try to kill it, but the small knife he possessed would take too much time to pierce the creature's thick hide, and he feared it would regain consciousness too soon for him to finish the job. He could see his own blood trickling from the beast's mouth, courtesy of the cut on his palm, which was bleeding more than he had expected.

Philip made a flash decision. Caution won out over his primal instincts and he decided to run while he had the chance. Leaving the troll in a giant heap on the ground, Philip staggered away at a shamble of a run. He almost lost his balance but steadied himself with his injured hand against the rock wall of the mountainside, leaving a smear of blood. He ran further, he ran hard, wondering what had made him think he could best a troll with just his fists. He shook his head. Stupid! He should never have given in to the urge to test himself against his trollish heritage.

Between one step and the next, as he headed back towards camp and Alayna, Philip had a chilling realization. Blood still seeped from his hand and dripped to the earth as he ran, leaving a trail of droplets for any hunter or predator to follow by sight and by scent. The troll would awaken soon and the beasts were notoriously vengeful creatures. He had been lucky to strike that stunning blow and doubted he'd be able to duplicate that feat with just his fists and small belt knife. He needed real weapons—tools he had left behind half a year gone when he quit his old profession as a Collector.

Philip's loss of blood was giving the troll a direct trail to track—a trail he was certain it would follow especially since it had already tasted his fresh blood. A rumbling howl of anger pierced the mountain air as if to punctuate his thoughts. The troll must have regained consciousness. Philip was the prey now and there was nothing he could do but run!

CHAPTER TWO

Beathan tossed the stolen bauble in the air and caught it nonchalantly. It was nothing of immense value, not worth more than a few pennies at most. But it was the act of stealing that he enjoyed, not the trinket itself. He strolled past a street waif who was crouched with his hands held out, waiting for any kind of gesture of pity. Beathan again tossed the shiny trinket into the air, only this time it landed in the boy's lap.

He winked at the lad and chuckled at the boy's astonishment. "Sell it, keep it. 'Tis yours now."

The waif gulped and muttered, "Generous you are sir, thank you kindly."

Beathan winked again and tousled the boy's unkempt hair. "No sir am I, lad." To emphasize the statement, he plucked at the torn and frayed sleeves on his tunic, so worn they lacked cuffs now, the ends ragged with wear.

He moved on, strutting with an insolent smile on his face, a grin meant to be seen by all those who recognized him for the gypsy that he was. Gypsies were not the most welcome of sorts. Mistrusted and feared, blamed for all manner of ills when they were nearby. If something went missing, it was bound to be the fault of the gypsies who were passing through the area. Most of the time, it was an unfair assessment of his kind.

Beathan smirked as he thought about how, in his case, it was usually true. He was a thief, and proud of it. The best thief he'd ever known. And folks weren't even aware he was part Fairy. Imagine their discomfort if that truth was known!

As he ambled through the throng, his gaze scanned the crowd for another pocket to pick, a purse to lift, or flashy jewelry to acquire. The market was lively even for this hour as evening approached.

Beathan was somewhere in England. Where exactly, he wasn't sure, but he'd long ago stopped trying to remember precisely where he was at all times. It was just so tiring. Much better to leave the mind free and clear to focus on important things.

Like mischief. Dancing was good too, or singing. Basically anything that celebrated the freedom to do what one wanted was a great way to pass the time. So he strolled through the market crowd and slipped his slender white fingers into a man's purse and removed just one coin. It was sometimes more difficult to steal only a portion of something rather than the whole of it. Delicately and deftly executed, Beathan flicked the coin end over end in celebration and then caught it again. Following his most recent victim, he crept lightly up behind the same man and replaced the coin just where he had taken it from—the purse. Putting back what you stole without getting caught was even more challenging than taking something in the first place. Beathan loved a challenge.

He skipped through the crowd on dancing feet, his rough spun breeches patched and ancient. Beathan wore a once-vibrant green vest over his tattered, cream tunic. The vest he had won off an old man, a man who had possessed it for too many years to count, leaving it spotted with grime and grease and dirt.

That had been a lucky night at dice, he thought, remembering how his winning streak had been good enough to literally win the clothes off his opponent's back. Well, luck had little to do with it, he admitted with a throaty chuckle that made passersby eye him nervously. One of Beathan's talents in life had always been his tricks. Why play fair when you could con or cheat and not get caught? His wrists, neck, and ears were covered with an array of mismatching jewelry that was mostly harmless, evidence of his loose interpretation of property ownership.

However, a few of his favorite pieces possessed charms, magical abilities that enabled the wearer to do something supernatural. His favorite was a bracelet, which acted as an amplifier of his own natural gifts. It had been stolen briefly last year by a half-mad bastard of a Guild member—Martin Astori—who'd been trying to inflict chaos on the world, using the bracelet to amplify his magic. But once it had been recovered, Beathan had returned to using it for its most common purpose —amplifying his speed.

As a half-fairy, his reflexes, quickness, and agility were inhuman and the bracelet only enhanced those traits. So on that night of gambling when he had won the vest from the old man, he simply tapped into the amplifying power of his bracelet as he rolled the dice, enabling him to move his hands fast enough to place the dice in exactly the position he desired with nobody the wiser. A person had to be careful when they cheated. Win too much and people began to suspect foul play, even if they couldn't prove their suspicions. However, Beathan had never been much for caution. He preferred a few bruises and a quick flight to playing life safe.

Twilight approached and the sky changed to the pastel in-between-time that marked the change from day to night. The moon began to show against a pale sky before it was fully dark, hinting at the coming night. Fairies loved the night. The moon and stars cast shadows that a normal eye wouldn't see, but they were lovely to the eyes of his kind. Beathan continued on his meandering path, stealing and then replacing more coins from purses, a bracelet from a woman's wrist, wares off vendors' tables, and even a hat from a man's head until he began to tire of stealing and then replacing stolen items.

He did nab a loaf of bread, which he kept, and gnawed on to appease his growling stomach. But nobody was perfect. Besides his saintly returns of all the stolen goods were not really for the benefit of the owners, it was his way of challenging his wits and abilities, keeping himself sharp. He had no qualms about keeping what he took.

However, tonight he couldn't shake the sense that something was missing. As he strolled and played the part of trickster, a discontentment grew inside. Usually a night of theft and mischief coupled with a semi-full stomach was enough to send him contentedly to his bed—or at least a leafy bed under a bush, that is. What was wrong? Why this feeling of dissatisfaction?

Beathan pondered his unsettled feelings for a while without reaching any clear conclusions, yet a vague idea began to form. Maybe his disillusionment with the evening was due to the fact that thievery wasn't anywhere as exciting as it used to be. He hadn't had a real adventure since he'd gained the wrinkles that marked his thin face and framed his hooknose. Last week he'd studied his appearance in a stolen hand mirror, gazing at the shock of dirty blond, wavy hair framing his face, and the twinkle in his eyes. Those attributes belied the wrinkles and lent a measure of youth to what would otherwise be the appearance of a man in his early middle years.

The wrinkles were not a problem in and of themselves. No real contradiction to his actual age—although for many years he had appeared younger than he was. What made the wrinkles noteworthy was that they had been gained through magic when Beathan had been forcibly linked, against his will, to the magician Astori. The madman had sucked some of the health and youth from Beathan, among other creatures.

That was the night Beathan had met Philip, which had led to the forging of an unlikely partnership in the face of Astori's betrayal of Philip and the Guild. Philip, the former Collector, and Beathan, the half-breed fairy, had joined forces to stop Astori from reigniting the Great Transformation—a period of history when the supernatural realm had enigmatically multiplied itself without following any of its normal conventions. During the Great Transformation people had fallen asleep human and woken up werewolves, vampires or worse, without a hint as to why their transformation had happened. Even an ill-behaved fairy like Beathan could see the problems inherent with that scenario.

After that night in New York, Philip ceased his collection of magical creatures, acknowledging the hypocrisy of doing so in contradiction to his own hybrid nature. Beathan could look back with a sense of satisfaction at having helped Philip gain that freedom of belief and the courage to change his course in life. They'd won a victory that night, but it had been hard fought and not without its price.

Beathan had often wondered how Alayna had adjusted to her new nature, and whether he might grow accustomed to the years of youth he himself had lost to the rogue, Guild magician, Martin Astori.

But that night was over and gone, why dwell on it now? Beathan forced his mind to turn to cheerier thoughts. He continued to wander through the maze of stalls and tents, trying to ignore the existential question of why he suddenly found his favorite pastime—theft—less interesting than usual.

He stopped suddenly when he came to the northeast corner of the market. This area had an almost carnival feel, with people dressed up in costumes. A small traveling troupe had set up a makeshift stage to perform who knew what ghastly rendition of one play or another.

Beathan cringed at what was sure to be less than a masterful performance. He was certain he could do much better than most at acting. But then, Beathan was much better than most people at almost everything, or at least so it had always seemed to him.

No, it was not the stage that caught his attention but something far more interesting and entirely more comical. It was trickery at its best. There were not many beings in the world that could match a half-breed fairy-gypsy like himself for chicanery, but a faun was one of the few. Fauns were deceptive, honey-tongued, and wily in the most dangerous fashion. They often had a dark streak also, forcing you to stay vigilant at all times, lest you become a victim of their trickery.

And their tricks were not always gentle. Beathan had once seen a wizened, old faun trick a nobleman into walking into quicksand just to repay the man for calling him ugly. Yet, all in all, Beathan liked fauns. Maybe not their personalities as such, but life around them remained interesting, never tedious. After all, when you were forced to constantly stay on your guard against a web of deception how could a person grow bored?

He slid to the back of the small crowd gathered to watch the faun. It appeared to be a woman in her late twenties, but that was a ruse, a web of magical lies spun by the spell-casting faun. It was the first and foremost trick of any faun—a concealment spell.

Looking like a goat on the bottom half of its body and often having horns attached to the head atop, a human torso was bound to draw attention. Fauns in their natural form stood out. This faun had decided to act the part of a woman tonight. Beathan chuckled as he watched it run its game on the local lord. The faun quickly picked Beathan out of the crowd with its keen eye for detail and they shared a stare of recognition.

Neither would reveal the other as more than human—as supernatural —for what would be the cause? Beathan smirked as he watched the faun go back to bewitching the lord out of his fortune in a series of games and challenges that appeared to be easy to win yet never yielded a successful result for the noble. The lord's temper was heating up with each loss but he was too blind to see the truth. It was magic that was beating him and fooling the crowd, not his own shortcomings, yet if a man was too ignorant of magic to spot its use, why then he deserved to be the victim! Besides, most lords in this land were rarely kind, or fair, or even decent at all. Beathan had no pity for any of them.

He watched for a time, enjoying the faun's ruse the way an audience enjoys a performance, laughing with the crowd as the noble lost yet again, and ahhing when the faun revealed where the winning move had been. The spectacle kept Beathan's attention for a time and allowed him to forget the strange empty feeling he had felt while thieving, a pastime that normally brought him good spirits.

The crowd cheered yet another victory by what they thought was a humble woman, when a flash of metal caught Beathan's eye. It was a ring on the finger of the lass to his right. Worth stealing? Not really, as it didn't look expensive. It was cheap copper, with an odd, dull rock set in it. Maybe granite. Either way, not a stone that would usually be used for jewelry. On face value, it was worth nothing more to Beathan than the excitement of daring to steal it. Yet, there was a pull that Beathan couldn't resist. He felt his eyes searching it out, staring against his will, until he took a few steps closer to the lass in order to get a better look, a clearer sense of what he was seeing.

Ah, yes! Realization and anticipation raced through him and Beathan's body thrummed with excitement. It was a charm! The stone-crested ring must conceal magical potential of some kind. It had been years since he discovered a new charm! Fate had brought him to an object capable of bringing back his spirits. In a heartbeat, he sidled up to the girl, slipped the ring from her finger and onto his own with his inhuman speed. Too easy. But as his favorite saying went, "Beggars should be stealers. A man makes his own luck." Beathan loved the reminder that 'easy' usually had to be worked for and earned. He had definitely earned the ease with which he stole after spending years honing his skills.

With the ring firmly on his finger, he turned to leave the crowd that was still watching the faun and its tricks. Beathan did so with a smile on his face and lightness in his heart. He glanced down at the plain ring adorning his finger. A feeling of almost uncontrollable glee bubbled up at the thought of all the tests and trials he would have to conduct to discover what charm this ring held. A quite desirable task.

However, the glee was short-lived. Suddenly, every nerve in his body felt tense, the way it did when danger was around. Beathan had never tried to understand his instincts. As much ask why water is wet or the moon is white. He simply trusted them. And now those self-same instincts told him to run, alerting him to danger. He scanned the marketplace and crowd as he made his way with deliberation towards the nearest exit.

A group of four men, on the edge of his vision, had started moving in his direction. Although they didn't appear to be looking at him, he could feel their collective gaze burning into his very skin. Dressed in all black, black boots, pants, and cloaks with hoods pulled up. A Guild look about them. Collectors! "Members of the hidden society that hunted all supernatural creatures using any means necessary."

Beathan cursed his inattentiveness due to his excitement at discovering the ring. He loved adventure. A little bit of danger made life worth living. But he also liked surviving. Staying alive meant staying aware, and he had neglected this cardinal rule while reveling in the faun's spectacle and the discovery of the charmed ring.

Beathan had forgotten the most important rule of all, "Don't be an idiot! Idiots end up dead." Stupid people didn't pay attention to their surroundings.

Flicking three of his rings in a particular order, he muttered a concealment charm to hide his jangles. Hopefully he would escape, but it was best to be prepared for all situations. He wouldn't want to end up captured without his spelled jewelry. With his charm cast, he turned a corner to sprint away with all his might. A good thief knew when to run. There was no shame in fleeing an unmatched fight.

Beathan took three quick steps before someone in a dark cloak stepped out of the shadows and bludgeoned him across the face with a club.

There was a sickening moment of pain and shock, then everything went dark.

CHAPTER THREE

"Well, you're not much to look at." The voice spoke in an accent that was difficult to place. The best Beathan could do to identify the accent was to discern that the person speaking was probably from east of here. Or maybe north. No, east.

Still groggy from the blow, Beathan pried opened his eyes and answered in his lilting brogue. "So sorry t' disappoint. I do always aim t' please." He attempted to flourish his hand just a little but the manacle attaching him to the wall was too short to allow it. The chain gave an annoying clank. Nothing worse than chains, especially those that kept a person locked tight. After a moment, he became more aware of his surroundings. He sat with his back against the wall, both of his wrists raised slightly above his head. The awkward position in which he had been slumped while unconscious had left him aching in unfamiliar places.

The rocking and shaking of the compartment, coupled with the fact that the floor underneath him felt wooden not stone, meant he found himself in some sort of prisoner transport. Probably a reinforced wagon of some kind. The Guild always had been proud of their gadgets and tools. It would be just like them to have a jail cell on wheels. Beathan filed away this information before turning his gaze towards the person with whom he was occupying the cell.

Relief flashed through him at the first glance. Elfas. Their kind had always been on good terms with his, the fairy folk, due to their kindred natures. Perhaps he'd found an ally. Beathan surreptitiously checked his rings and jewelry, the charms he'd conveniently concealed just before his capture. They weren't invisible exactly, but the spell simply encouraged the average eye to pass over them, viewing them as another part of the arm, neck, or finger on which they rested.

A second and stronger wave of relief washed through Beathan, a tingle all the way down to his bones. His jangles were safe, and most importantly, the spelled jewelry was still with him. He thanked whatever there was to thank in this universe that he'd had that last second of foresight to hide his most precious possessions. Perhaps it would make up for his lack of attention in allowing himself to be caught. Disgust at his capture made his mouth puckered up as if tasting something sour.

"Bad taste in your mouth?" the Elfas inquired politely, although there seemed to be a smirk hiding just behind his eyes waiting to emerge. Something about the Elfas reminded Beathan of a man wearing a mask.

"Surely is," Beathan responded. He wasn't about to divulge what he had really been thinking—private thoughts, thoughts of disdain for himself and his predicament. Twice now in the span of less than a year he had found himself captured! What was the world coming to if a life-long escape artist such as Beathan could no long expect to stay out of the brig?

No, wait, brig was for ships, wasn't it? What was the fancy word for a jail cell when a body was on land? He didn't have a chance to finish his rambling thought process as the Elfas spoke again.

"So, what did they grab you for, Fairy? Theft? Tricksome-ness?" The Elfas spoke very precisely, enunciating every syllable of every word. He spoke English perfectly but it was as if he was aware of the accent he possessed and made up for it by making absolutely certain that he did not slur or mumble anything he said. He also seemed to think he was clever, with his guesses and with his way of expressing those conjectures. Beathan had always been a thief and he was not ashamed of it. He had always been fairly crafty, as well. But it wasn't polite to point that out to a person.

"The name's Beathan. An' actually no..." He elongated the pause waiting for the Elfas to supply his name in return. He did after a moment's hesitation.

"Azir." The Elfas nodded his head in greeting, so that his straight, black hair fell forward slightly covering his thin, almost hollow features. He was pale of skin, and that was normal for the Elfas, but his hair and eyes were darker than most Beathan had previously seen. Many of the

Elfas, Alfur, or Alderfolk—however you called them—were fair of hair and eyes to match their fair skin.

"Well, actually no, Azir, they didn't. Just so ya' know, I was hardly doin' anything discourteous, me bein' the soul of good manners and all. When out o' nowhere some fellow in a dark cloak beats me over the side o' me head un-gentleman-like."

Azir really did smirk this time. "Of course." He clearly didn't believe Beathan.

What are the odds Beathan thought, that of all the times I've made mischief, I get arrested the one time when I haven't done anything? And my co-captive won't even believe me. It was ironic enough to muster a pained laugh from him.

"Something funny, friend?" Azir asked. The way he said friend, told Beathan that he was uncertain of whether or not that was true.

"Nothing worth repeatin', mate." Beathan noticed the Elfas' face darken slightly as if he thought Beathan was laughing at him. Touchy fellow.

"How fascinating. I had heard about the Irish accent, but now, hearing it in person it is quite astounding, formidable rather. It is clearly not something that can be taught." The Elfas emphasized the word taught.

"Oh, we have our schoolin' as much as the next lad, but me folks never laid much importance on formal education. Always thought a man learned better with his hands than strictly his head." Beathan answered.

Azir made an attempt to raise his hands in apology, but seeing as he was chained to the wall like Beathan, all he managed to do was show his palms. "Truly, I did not mean that as an insult. It was merely an observation." The wagon rattled on, causing clinks of metal from their chains to punctuate the conversation.

Beathan inclined his head in acceptance. Sure you didn't, he thought to himself. Something told him it was exactly the way the Elfas had intended the comment to be taken about the Irish accent lacking education. Why, he was not sure, but he was certain that his companion was hiding a lot more behind that polite façade than he let on. Nevertheless, Beathan tried to put the comment behind him. He'd been called a bumpkin before and would likely be again. People deemed Beathan unlearned and ignorant at their own peril. He decided to be polite and try to ascertain more about his prison companion through small conversation.

"Well, we've firmly established that I'm from the Fair Isle. An' you? Where do ya' hail from?"

Azir paused as if wondering whether or not to respond. Finally, he did. "From the east," was all he would say, spoken in his proper, yet heavily accented voice. Now that he admitted it outright, Beathan could definitely pick up the sound of Eastern Europe in his language.

For a time, neither of them spoke and Beathan simply observed Azir. Black hair, silky straight, hung just below his jawline, and no doubt it covered elegantly pointed ears. Narrow features framed hollow, dark eyes —a midnight blue. The Elfas had a regal look to him, and an imperious manner, as if he expected those around him to do as he commanded.

His fellow captive wore close fitting, black hose with black leather boots of quality cut. The tunic was a gloomy forest green, the color of deep woods on a sunless day. All together, an impressive attire.

Azir noticed him observing his appearance and smiled. Something about the smile was not altogether friendly. It wasn't as if Beathan thought the Elfas intended to be contrary, but the fellow had an air about him that Beathan found unsettling. Perhaps it was nothing. After all, he had met many of Azir's kind before and had grown to be friends. Meetings of any supernatural creatures took place beyond the realm of men, and any first meetings that occurred were always punctuated by caution. It was the way it had to be. Maybe that was all there was to his reaction. Beathan had found himself in a terrible predicament with a complete stranger. He was likely to mistrust anyone in this situation.

Deciding to break the long silence, Beathan asked, "So, what about you? Do ya' have a tale of capture worthy o' spinnin'?"

"It is not much of a tale to recount. I was... conducting an experiment, through which I grew to be incapacitated. It was during my unfortunate, weakened state that our 'un-gentlemen-like' captors, as you so eloquently put it, happened upon me." Azir paused and lifted his nose disdainfully at the mention of his jailers. Beathan ignored the dig at his description of the Collectors from earlier.

"Well, tis no shame t' be captured. After all, ya' can say ya' shared a jail cell with the most uncatchable thief in all o' Britain." Beathan tried to lighten the mood.

"Uncatchable?"

"Well, 'til now, that is." Beathan laughed ruefully and for the first time Azir smiled genuinely. There wasn't any change in his features from the other smiles that Beathan had seen, yet somehow Beathan was sure that this time it was different.

Perhaps I am being overly cautious, he thought. We probably both are. Maybe there's a partnership waiting for me with this one yet. If Beathan did partner up with the Elfas and work to escape, it would not be the most peculiar partnership he'd had.

His thoughts turned to Philip then, and Alayna. He hoped the one-time Collector had succeeded in staying clear of his former employers and was enjoying a free life—a life not spent continually hunting his own kind. Philip did have a lovely lady besotted with him. Not many a man could ask for more than that in life.

Man? Why am I thinking that way, he laughed to himself. Half-breeds walked the line between the human world and the supernatural but were hardly in either. If anything, he found more acceptance from his fairy kin —although, even they looked at him strangely, at times, because of his human side. He hoped Alayna had found greater acceptance among her new family, the Elfas.

Alayna.

Thinking of her sparked another thought. A dangerous thought, but not dangerous for him. His own situation couldn't get any worse.

Alayna. Alayna was now one of the Alderfolk. Beathan had heard rumors about their kind that might be useful now.

"Azir, I have heard... things about the Elfas."

Azir tilted his head slightly to the side, waiting in silence for Beathan to continue. The soul of patience.

"Interestin' things. About powers that could be o' help t' us." He raised his eyebrows suggestively to the Elfas sitting across from him. Azir's hands were hitched up to the wall of the wagon, and he was slumped into an awkward position against the wall, yet somehow he managed to make it look kingly, as if he wanted to be exactly where he was.

Beathan didn't often grow jealous. In fact, he literally couldn't remember the last time he had felt the stirrings of envy in his heart. But he couldn't help but wish he had the same poise as the Elfas across from him. Instead, he felt a cramp forming in his shoulder.

Azir furrowed his brow. "Do you not think that if I could do something to get myself out of this predicament that I would have done so already? Besides most of... my people's abilities are not of much use when one is chained and in a cage." He rattled the manacles bitterly to prove his point.

Beathan stiffened. Interestingly, he'd said 'his people' as if they were not his people. He was as strange an Elfas as Beathan had ever met. They were an interconnected species. Most were more attached to their distant cousins than a human was to its parents.

Azir continued. "We are a people of nature, of wind and rain. I am a creature of... moonlight and stars, not metal and wheels. I can do nothing more than you. In fact, I suspect you might have more to offer for an escape than me judging by those charms you wear."

Odd. Beathan felt sure that Azir had been about to say sunlight but instead switched the word to moonlight. He responded to the creature of the Alderfolk sitting across from him in an instinctive, careful manner.

"What charms?" How had Azir seen through his concealment spell? It wasn't common for his spells to work on some, like the Collectors who had captured them for instance, but not others.

Azir grinned slyly. "Please, do not try to play me the fool. I have studied magic of all kinds. I like... new experiences, and magic often provides an interesting diversion. But I have never seen someone wear more than one charmed item. And yet, here you are wearing many."

He emphasized the word 'many'. The Elfas had a tendency to emphasize odd words. It gave his speech a calculated sound, made it appear as if he always knew something more, or possessed some secret knowledge.

Beathan waited, willing to volunteer nothing more about his powers. Why should he open up about his abilities if Azir would not do the same about his own powers?

"What do they do?" The Elfas asked curiously. "What does that one do? The bracelet." His eyes trailed almost hungrily up to the amplifying bracelet Beathan wore. He spoke again in a whisper before Beathan could answer. "I do so love new experiences." It was almost as if he were now speaking to himself. However, he seemed to snap out of his reverie, and his dark eyes focused in on Beathan's.

The fairy decided to avoid the question again and stayed silent, meeting the eye contact with a furrowed brow. He saw frustration grow in Azir's eyes.

"Tell me, what does it do?" Azir spoke again, his voice forceful and yet almost a purr. It was strangely hypnotic the way he spoke. "Tell. Me. Now."

Beathan felt his mind softening and growing groggy again, just slightly, and he opened his mouth to answer almost before the words had left Azir's mouth, but then the Elfas let out a wracking cough, as if utilizing vocal chords that had long been unused.

Whatever magic the Elfas had created in the moment was gone, disappearing because of the interruption, and Beathan felt a strengthening of his will to resist. Azir looked confused. Almost dazed, as if he wasn't sure what had just happened. Altogether, Beathan wasn't sure what had happened either. He had never heard that the Alderfolk—Alfur as they were known in parts of the Northern regions like Iceland—had the power to bend the minds of others to their will.

"I'll thank ya' kindly not t' be so nosy." Beathan said when the moment settled. "What I wear o' don't wear be none o' your concern."

He saw a dark gleam of recognition flicker through Azir's eyes, as if something had just crossed his mind, something he understood. Beathan wondered what it was, but he didn't ask because he was sure the Elfas wouldn't tell him. Instead he just watched the lean Elfas across from him give that secretive smile again.

"That is fair enough. I must apologize for my actions. It was terribly crude of me to try and bully answers out of you. Please forgive me and blame it on my confinement." Azir spoke words dripping honey but Beathan wasn't at all convinced.

"Well, back t' you then," Beathan directed the conversation, "I've heard the Elfas can communicate mind t' mind or some such. S'that truth?"

"Yes, we can to a certain extent."

"I happen t' know a lass just like you who might be worth contactin', if ya' had a mind t' do so."

Azir shook his head. "I hardly think she could help us. Nor is she just like me. Not many are." He said the last bit as if to himself.

"Couldn't hurt now, could it?" Beathan asked again.

"What makes you believe that she could be of any use to us? We are here and she is not. We will likely be in St. Thomas's before long, and you know as well as I, that anyone captured and taken there does not return. Ever. Who is she that you know her so well as to believe she would try to rescue you, and yet care for her so little that you would knowingly ask her to undertake an assault on St. Thomas's and face certain failure. Failure that would result in her capture." Azir tilted his head in question.

"Tis not who she is t' me, but rather who she knows."

Beathan grinned craftily the way he did when he saw a great ruse to be played on someone. This time it was the ultimate target—the Collectors Guild. He couldn't think of a better victim of his cleverness than those arrogant, holier-than-thou Collectors. Although to be honest, it wouldn't be his cleverness or guile that saved him. It would be Philip's.

"Trust me," Beathan said, "She's worth contactin'."

Azir stared at him for a long moment with shrewd eyes. Finally, he nodded. "Alright. I'll try." He paused to stare at Beathan, "But we work together in this. We escape together. I'll not have you use me and then leave me to rot."

Beathan nodded his acceptance. The Elfas might be hiding something, but anything had to be better than becoming a permanent resident of the supernatural prison that was St. Thomas's.

The Elfas gave a grim smile at Beathan's acceptance of his terms. "Who is she?"

"Alayna. She's one o' your kind—the Alderfolk. Although, she's... new to the species."

"New?" Azir stared at Beathan sharply. "My kind do not replicate by turning others the way some species do. And if she is naught more than a babe, she cannot help us."

"'Tis much too long a story t' recount now. Ya' have t' trust me. She's one o' you, an' she's new. An' who she's with can help us. Besides, what have ya' got t' lose by tryin'?"

"Very well." Azir seemed to accept that he wouldn't be getting answers right now. "But I would very much like to hear this story at a later point."

"Agreed." Beathan would tell that story and many more if they could just slip away from their captors.

The Elfas closed his eyes and stretched his fingers wide and then closed them into fists, then wide again, then closed again. It was almost as if he were trying to pump blood through his body more quickly. Beathan had no magic such as mind-to-mind contact so he didn't feel the need to ask what was happening. It was not likely he'd understand any answers given anyway.

"What does she look like? What does she act like?" Azir demanded imperiously.

"Name's Alayna. Strawberry blonde hair. Pointy ears just like ya' got on that thin head o' yours. Beautiful, peaceful, yet I believe there's quite a fighter lurking beneath the calm exterior." Beathan rattled off anything he could think of about Alayna to the Elfas. He didn't really know her that well and he had only seen her once in the half a year since they had initially parted company.

"That is enough. Be silent."

Azir kept his eyes closed and Beathan watched him screw up his face in effort. What exactly he was doing or how he was doing it was unclear. The silence stretched on for five minutes, then ten.

After at least twenty minutes of Azir and his scrunched up face, Beathan was about to speak, to ask how it was going, but the Elfas opened his eyes and Beathan saw real exhaustion in them. Maybe he had accomplished something after all. Leastwise he had tried, of that much Beathan was certain.

"It is done. At least done to the best of my abilities," Azir said. What he meant by that, Beathan wasn't sure.

"Difficult, eh?"

Azir nodded wearily. "Reaching mind to mind is much easier when close to the subject. She is far away, your friend. North of here by many miles and many days of travel. And I am not as good at this type of contact as I once was."

The wagon clattered to a halt.

"I hope it is time for some food," Azir murmured. "The rigor of that mental exercise has made me famished."

Beathan was about to respond when the doors opened, sending brilliant light shining into the gloom in which they were chained. It half blinded his eyes.

"Too much talking." A gruff voice said to them. "If you can't shut up, we'll have to shut you up."

A club was raised and all Beathan could think in glum resignation was: 'not again!' before the weapon began its downward stroke toward his temple, landing with cracking impact that sent him into the oblivion of unconsciousness.

The last thing Beathan was aware of before the darkness took him was Azir's strangely dark eyes peering at him hungrily. The Elfas was muttering to himself as he watched Beathan. His words made Beathan suddenly and abnormally grateful for the chains that were separating them and keeping his companion restrained.

Azir's voice punctuated Beathan's last coherent thought saying, "Not hungry. I was wrong before. I'm... thirsty."

CHAPTER FOUR

Philip ran, his heart pounding in his ears and blood pumping through his veins. He was tired from the confrontation with the troll, but adrenalin kept him going. One foot in front of the other, he slid and slipped downhill and out of the high peaks. Trolls were strong and powerful beings, so it had probably rebounded from their encounter quicker than Philip. Yet, trolls were not particularly fast. Persistent and vengeful, yes, they could hold a scent for days at a time if they chose. But they often caught their prey because of that persistence, not through outright speed.

So he ran, ran hard enough that he must have opened a steady lead on the creature. After all, Philip could weave his way through slim openings and squeeze between trees on the narrow game trails that the troll would have difficulty following. Sometimes he thought he heard the crashing sound of some huge beast thrashing its way through the trees behind him, but he was never sure if it was his imagination or not. So he kept running and didn't look back.

For good measure he wove his trail back and forth across the hills on which he was descending. He crossed streams and raced up or down those small bodies of water to cover his scent. He didn't think it would be enough to fully shake the raging predator in pursuit, but it would slow the creature down as it was forced to stop and ascertain where exactly its prey had left the water.

In time it would find his trail again and continue the hunt, but perhaps his evasive maneuvers would buy Philip enough time to reach Alayna, break their camp in the foothills, and then make for the coast. Odds were, even a furious troll probably wouldn't venture into civilized territory.

Philip and Alayna had no such qualms. Philip looked entirely human —his supernatural characteristics were not a matter of physical appearance. With Alayna, all they had to do was keep her hood up to cover her thinner and more angular, elegant features. At the very least, she could likely pass for human as long as she kept her golden red hair pulled forward to cover her delicately pointed ears. Those ears were a dead giveaway that she wasn't a normal woman.

But if she hid them, most humans were too polite to mention her difference in appearance. Likely they would just chalk her looks up to some beautiful and exotic origin. Humans had a way of rationalizing what they didn't understand. Funny how easy it was to think of them as humans and himself as something else. Not long ago that hadn't been the case. Philip could remember vividly his desperate fight to cling to his humanity, to convince himself that he was a simple man and nothing more. Well, he might look simple, with his plain brown hair hanging loosely and uncut around his head, and his average features that wouldn't make anyone look twice at him in a crowd, but anyone who crossed paths with Philip in a fight could attest otherwise. His strength and stamina clearly did not match his slender frame.

Philip pushed himself harder. *Alayna will never let me hear the end of this,* he thought with a grimace. *She had enjoyed our time in these mountains. And now we have to leave, all because I poked the monster.* He expelled a huge gust of air in exertion but also in frustration and ran on.

By the time Philip neared their camp he was fairly certain that he had built up enough of a lead on the troll to grab a moment of rest. With the faint smell of wood smoke in the air from their campfire he stumbled his way in exhaustion through the trees that surrounded their camp.

As he entered their temporary—and soon to be old—home, Alayna looked up from the small spit she was turning. On it was the carcass of a rabbit, crackling and brown, and dripping with juice. It looked beyond delicious.

"I was wondering where you'd gone." Alayna tilted her head to the side and narrowed her eyes to appraise his disheveled appearance before continuing. "I considered following your trail and catching up with you wherever you went, but now I think I'm glad I didn't. What did you do, fight with a bear?"

"Worse," Philip gasped trying to speak but finding it difficult due to his burning lungs. "We have to leave. Now."

To her credit, she took him at his word. In one swift motion she kicked dirt over the fire to smother the flames, grabbed their packs off the ground—which they kept filled and ready to leave at a moment's notice—and tossed his to him.

Philip caught his light travel pack with a grunt and slung it over his shoulder. Alayna did the same with hers. She might be even more slender than Philip, but she was no longer human. Her body was lean and hard, and also soft in all the right places. Philip shook his head to clear it of that line of thinking. No room for lustful thoughts right now, not with an angry troll in hot pursuit.

As a last act before breaking camp, Alayna reached down for the rabbit she'd been spit roasting but Philip stopped her.

"No, leave it. It's a long shot, but maybe it'll be enough to buy us even a little bit more time. Every minute helps."

Alayna didn't respond at first, she just left the rabbit dripping juices into the dirt that covered where the fire had been. But she did shake her head.

And finally, she had to ask.

"What did you do this time, Philip?" Alayna rolled her eyes at him in exasperation.

"This time?" Philip responded, striving for a measure of indignation.

"Yes, this time," she said in a measured tone. "Last time you stole a kill from a mountain lion and we had to fight or leave, and we didn't want to kill the animal for no reason so we left. The time before that you picked a fight with a werewolf who wandered into our camp."

"He tried to bite you. It was a full moon!"

"It was not a full moon, Philip, it was a day from full at least," she said primly.

Philip snorted. She always did try to spin a situation.

Alayna bore on without stopping. "And the time before that you tried to kick a Wight out of its cave for the night."

Philip pursed his lips. She did have a point but there wasn't time to argue his side of things now. Little good it would do to point out that there had been a ferocious storm brewing and the cave that had housed the Wight had been the only shelter for miles. They had needed that cave.

Besides, Wights were half dead anyway so a little cold and rainy weather wouldn't have harmed it at all. But Philip didn't say any of that now because they needed to leave immediately, not debate whether those incidents had occurred due to reason or his wild nature.

"Well, this time it's worse my love. We have to move now."

"What did you do, Philip?"

"Picked a fight with a troll for no good reason and now it's mad as hell and on my trail—our trail now. So we have to leave, right away." Philip finally felt like his wind was back in his lungs. Maybe a little argument had been good because it had given him the respite he'd needed.

"How long do we have?" Alayna was all business now. There were no more exasperated remarks about his conduct.

Truly the events of last winter had changed her in more ways than just her physical appearance, more than just her race. The shy, timid, and peaceful lady he had fallen in love with in the New York countryside had become a strong, capable, confident—if slightly bossy—woman.

Well, not a woman exactly. Not a woman at all really. She was one of the Elfas, or Alderfolk, as they were known in the Americas. Their race was nimble and lithe, forest dwellers and tree climbers. Swift runners with a passion for nature and for their kin and family, a largely peaceful race of beings, but they would fight to protect their own.

Alayna's transformation had been one of the side effects of their fight to defeat the rogue Guild agent Martin Astori. It was odd to think of him as a rogue member of the Guild. Wasn't that what Philip was now?

He ignored this dangerous line of thought and answered Alayna's question. "Half hour, maybe an hour at most. If we leave now and we push hard, we can hopefully build up even more of a lead on the creature. I'd like to try and make it to civilization and avoid another confrontation."

"I should think so, another altercation might be the death of you," she said eyeing his tattered, beat up appearance with a grin and wink. She always did know how to make him smile. He grinned back at her.

"Well, if we hope to avoid impending doom, we'd better get going."

They turned in unison and began taking long, steady strides away from camp and down the mountain. They mediated their pace so as not to exhaust themselves, aware without speaking that they needed to keep up this pace for more than a day, perhaps two, before they were out of the wilderness and near enough to a city to force the troll to relinquish the hunt. They weren't likely to shake their pursuer before such a time.

Here I am, Philip thought, bringing trouble and danger down on Alayna. Yet, that notion didn't bring him the worry or discomfort it once had. Of course, he still had the need to protect her. He loved Alayna, she was his whole world. But he had come to realize that she was brave and resilient. She would not easily break.

They ran for some time before either of them spoke.

Finally, Alayna broke the silence. "Why did you stalk a troll to its den and decide to pick a fight with it, Philip?" Her serious voice.

He could tell she was curious and really did want to know. Sighing, Philip wondered how to make her understand the urges he struggled with on a daily basis, without sounding completely insane.

He spent a few moments gathering his thoughts before responding. She gave him time to think. They had been around each other long enough to know what the other needed.

Eventually Philip managed to answer. "I guess I wanted to see how I matched up to it. I am part troll, after all. It sort of felt like I was measuring myself against my heritage." He gave an inward groan. It did sound crazy. Who picked a fight with a ten-foot troll? Idiots, that's who. So what did that make Philip?

"I see," Alayna responded. It was clear she did not really see and how could Philip expect her to?

He tried again, explained as best as he could. "Last winter you changed, Alayna, you became something totally new—a whole new being. But I changed too. I may have the same capabilities and potential that I've had since I was a child, but I wasn't utilizing them. I never allowed myself to be anything other than human—a safe, conservative, cautious human."

A part of him rebelled at the idea that any normal human being would have considered his previous profession as a Collector as 'safe' or 'cautious', but in comparison to the wilder tendencies he exhibited now, that's how it felt.

They ran a few more steps before Alayna again said, "I see."

This time she really did sound like she was beginning to understand. In that moment, Philip loved her all over again. She really did understand him. He supposed that spending all day, every day, with a person made it easier to understand them, but either way, he wasn't about to take it for granted. She was a marvelous person.

"I think some of my reckless behavior is due to me testing my limits. How far can I give in to my untamed side, my wild nature before it's too far? Alayna, you only have one nature now, you're one of the Elfas. But I'm a half-breed, a hybrid, and my nature feels divided sometimes. I guess I'm just trying to sift through all the emotions that have come with yielding to my inhuman status. Trying to figure myself out."

Philip shrugged, uncomfortable. It wasn't that he didn't like being vulnerable with Alayna, she knew all of his deepest places, the good and the bad. But this was different. As he spoke, Philip realized that he wasn't entirely in control, that he didn't fully know who he was. He was much closer than he had been when he'd fully denied his wild side, yet still he was searching to find the balance in his life.

Alayna laid a hand on his arm and pulled him gently to a halt. "I do understand, Philip." The love in her eyes was enough to drown a man. "And I'll be right here by your side every step of the way."

Then she pulled his face to hers and every thought in his head was lost in the glory of the moment. There were few things in life more blissful than kissing her. Her mouth was warm and wet in just the right way. Her tongue was gentle and firm. Her body lean and strong, yet supple against his as he pulled her close. She was a flurry of beautiful contradictions. They stood there for a timeless moment then broke apart.

Without another word they clasped hands and ran on again together. More together than they had been a moment ago, although if someone had told Philip that would be the case, he would not have believed it to be possible.

———

THEIR JOURNEY out of the mountains and towards civilization took the rest of the day, all through the night, and into the next morning. They pushed the pace enough to maintain the slim lead they had on the troll. By the time dawn's grey light was cresting the tops of the mountains behind them, they were nearing the end of their trek.

Philip's breath came in short gasps, his legs felt like lead. His sides still ached from the troll's cruel grasp. His fight with the troll yesterday had led into him returning to camp as swiftly as possible. He hadn't really rested since the night before when he had awoken early and snuck away from their camp to embark on his trip into the peaks where the troll lived. So when he saw a city opening up ahead of them through a break in the trees, he could hardly contain his relief.

"Just a few more minutes and we should be in the clear," he grunted to Alayna.

She nodded, not having any difficulty breathing. Her kind had nearly endless stamina. He on the other hand, had strength, power, and the gift of healing quickly among other abilities, but the potential to run for days on end was not one of those attributes.

They worked their way down the path in front of them, the trail easing up as it flattened out after leaving the last foothill. It was not long before they were slowing to a walk and stepping into the small city before them.

Trondheim was a port along the coast of Norway. It was situated on one of the many fjords that cut through the coastline in gorgeous fashion. The fjords looked like someone had swung an enormous sword at the earth and torn huge, long gouges out of the land, allowing the sea to flow into them.

Although they reminded Philip of the remnants of sword strokes, there was nothing ugly about them. Green patterned the slopes and the rocky promenades acted like bastions of the wild refusing to be tamed by the civilization. Fish and wildlife teemed in the fjords and seabirds of all kinds could be seen gliding through the air above them. Everything about the fjords reminded Philip of life. He had traveled with Alayna throughout this northern land over the last half year and he had seen many a shoreline and deserted fjord to be admired.

This fjord, instead, boasted a harbor full of ships to go with its natural beauty. Wood houses were intermingled with some of stone. Most were their natural colors, but a few had been painted red. The paint was faded and chipped. Philip imagined the weather in winter was enough to strip much of the color from their walls. They strode further into the city, making towards the water.

Alayna wrinkled her nose at the smell of the wharfs as they entered the port and walked along its dirty, cobblestoned streets. "Not exactly my favorite smell on earth," she murmured.

"Oh, I don't know," Philip disagreed. "I always rather liked the smell of the sea and ships. A harbor always felt like a very happening place to me. Lots going on." He couldn't help but feel nostalgic for his old Guild partner, James. They had sailed most of the Atlantic during the years that they had worked together, bagging almost every type of supernatural being there was to hunt.

"It smells like dead fish," she answered with a smile. "I always hated it when you showed up at my cottage smelling like you'd just bathed in harbor water." Alayna reached up and put a hand familiarly, affectionately on the back of his head and grasped a handful of his hair to pull him close for a kiss.

The contact was brief, but tender. Then she pulled away with a satisfied little groan. "Yes, indeed. You smell so much better now, love. Like clean sweat and pine needles and wood smoke. Like the forest in summer."

"I'm glad you approve." He smiled.

Philip would do just about anything to make Alayna happy and if smelling like a forest somehow pleased her, he was not about to complain. Besides, he was more at home in the woods now than he had ever been before accepting his true, split nature.

This feeling of nostalgia for ships and fish, for sailors and the smell of tar and bilge, was just that—nostalgia, a way to remember the past. Philip let himself remember and smiled at the thought of his old partner.

James would be glad that he was happy. He had always been pestering Philip to find a woman and settle down. Well, he had indeed found someone worthy of loving, although whether or not they had settled down was another question entirely.

He grinned at his last thought. He couldn't imagine the Alayna of today every being described as 'settled down'. She was as free a spirit as ever existed. The Elfas were one with nature, traversing the land through the wildest patches of earth that existed. They were not fighters by nature, but neither did they avoid adventure. No, Alayna was definitely not 'settled'.

They sat down on a lip of stone that faced the harbor to discuss what they might do next. Their entire plan had consisted of reaching Trondheim since the troll was likely clever enough to avoid such a heavy settlement of humans, and would not follow them within the city limits. They were safe for the moment. Trolls were impetuous and rash in their decisions, but not stupid. They might harry a lone farmstead on occasion, snatching a sheep or a pig for a quick and easy meal, but they knew to avoid cities.

The world of humans and the realm of magic and mythical creatures did not mix well. Blood was often shed, and while on average more human life was lost, in the end, those creatures that drew too much attention to themselves had a way of ending up dead. Whether that was at the hands of an angry mob of humans who didn't know exactly what they were facing, but were too enraged or afraid to avoid it any longer, or the more stealthy and quiet clutches of the Collectors Guild, either way, the creature was just as dead.

"Well, here we are. What did you have in mind now?"

"I didn't really think this far ahead." Philip uttered a rueful chuckle in response. "I was so preoccupied with not becoming a meal to be shoved down a troll's gullet that I didn't really think of what would come next. I figured we could decide together."

"Fair enough. Well, we can't leave the town by land any time soon because that troll will likely be snuffling around the edge of the city limits for days hoping to catch our scent." Alayna trailed off in annoyance as she saw where her train of thought was leading.

Philip grinned with mirth. It was the logical course of action and it would be fun to watch her squirm for a few days. "Looks like it's a sea passage for us then, doesn't it?" He spoke brightly as if not aware of her dislike for ships and their smells.

She rolled her eyes playfully back at him. "Fine," she said in mock exasperation. She was a good sport even when thrust into a situation she didn't like.

Philip laughed again at her expression reflecting over-annoyance. She was putting on a good act. "Oh, come now love, the high seas are not nearly so bad as you claim. The worst of the smells will be long gone a scarce few minutes after we leave port. Before you know it, you'll have the salty spray in your hair and a wind in your face..." Philip trailed off remembering the freedom that came on open water.

"You really do love it, don't you?" Alayna gave him a knowing smile. "The ocean, the water." She trailed a delicate hand lazily in a grand sweeping gesture of the harbor. "All of it."

"I did," Philip replied, turning serious. "But now it's more of a good memory than a desire to relive it. I'll sail when it's necessary, and while it's necessary I'll enjoy it. And after, I'll enjoy the freedom of the wilderness with you."

Alayna smiled fondly as if she was about to say something but instead she ended up clutching her head and gasping in the shock of sudden pain. She doubled over and Philip was at her side in a heartbeat, hands on her back trying to ascertain what was the problem.

"Alayna! Alayna, what's wrong?"

No answer. Instead the Elfas dropped to the ground and curled up in a tight ball, as if fighting a scream trying to pierce its way from her throat.

"Alayna, speak to me! Tell me what I can do!" Still no answer and Philip was forced to watch in anguish as she lay on the dirty cobblestones grunting and grasping her head in some kind of agony he couldn't understand or dispel.

It went on and on, Philip struggling with panic and fear, yet all he could do was sit with her in the grime of the street and hold her head in his lap as she fought down the screams.

Finally, blessedly, it was over. From one moment to the next she went from clutching her head and writhing in pain to grabbing him and burying her face in his chest and weeping in sweet relief at her ended torture.

Philip waited to ask questions. He let her tears dampen his shirt and her muffled sobs reach his ears until eventually they quieted and she was only breathing in gusty gasps. Finally, she pulled her face off his chest and looked up at him.

"What was that, love?" He asked as gently as he could.

"I'm not exactly sure," her voice quavered and he could tell she was still not over the shock of the intense pain she had been forced to endure.

He stayed silent until she was ready to speak again.

Alayna sat up beside him, her movements telling him she had begun to recover. She laid her head on his shoulder and spoke quietly, in an almost detached voice. "It was not completely unlike the gestalt consciousness my people possess. The oneness of mind we can achieve." *You know the way we can speak mind to mind with those we are intimate with.*

Her voice echoed in the silent privacy of his mind. He always felt a tingling warmth when she spoke through her mind to him. He could not return in kind, he did not possess that capability, but it made him feel close to her, nevertheless.

She continued. "But between those of my kind who we are not as close with, the oneness is not so much speaking mind to mind as it is the sharing of emotions, sensations, images that paint a picture. This can just as easily communicate what you need, yet without words."

"I see," Philip said, although he wasn't sure where she was going with her thoughts.

"This was like that shared oneness of mind, the nonverbal mental communication... only it was accompanied by pain, lots of it." She hiccupped a laugh that was half sob as she tried to shrug off the terrible ordeal.

"Why would it hurt?" Philip asked.

"I don't know."

"Who sent the message?"

"One of my kind, I believe. It had to be. But, I do not know why I would feel such pain! That has never happened before." Alayna was clearly as confused as he was.

Philip was worried. Why had this happened? Watching Alayna suffer hurt him in ways no troll ever could. They had to get to the bottom of it. They needed answers.

"Can you tell me nothing then, my love?" He asked, stroking her hair.

Alayna hesitated. There was something she had held back until now. He could see it in her eyes.

She spoke. "Well, the pain wasn't the only difference between this oneness of mind and the way it usually happens among the Elfas. There was also a dirtiness to it, a soiled feeling when our minds touched. Yet, it was strangely compelling also." She trailed off and stared at the street on which they were sitting, the grime of the cobblestones rubbing off on her brown leggings that she wore with her fitted brown tunic.

Philip was about to ask another question when she held his gaze with a grim look on her face. "That's not all, Philip."

Philip's gut clenched at her solemn expression. What could she have to tell him that was worse than what he had just witnessed happen?

"I saw Beathan. He was chained to a wall, in some sort of small wooden room. It looked like the room was moving." She paused and scrunched up her face trying to remember it all. "It all came in weird flashes. It wasn't a steady connection between our minds, whoever it was. Beathan chained to a wall flashed in my mind. Beathan talking, making a joke, which would be normal, only on his face was an ugly, purple bruise. Then it was just a vision of what had to be their captors, cloaked men, with weapons and then a wagon."

Philip squinted at the deceptively bright grayness of the sky above the port. What could it all mean? "I didn't know you could contact specific people over long distances." It had to have been specific, targeted. What were the odds that Beathan would have a fellow prisoner who had the capability of accidentally contacting Alayna's mind?

"We can't, not usually. It's very hard to target a specific person over long range. Especially when you don't know them. And I'm certain I didn't know this Elfas."

Philip nodded at her comment trying to put the pieces together.

"Philip, when I saw a flash of the captors, I saw a silver knife on one of their belts." Alayna looked fearfully into his eyes.

It had to be. They both knew what that meant, and it was really the only thing that made sense. The Guild had Beathan. Somehow he had allowed himself to be caught by Collectors and was being transported to St. Thomas's.

"They have him." Philip didn't have to elaborate on who he meant by 'they'. Alayna knew about whom he was talking. Pain etched his voice. He cared about Beathan. It hurt knowing he was a prisoner.

"We do not know why he was taken—for what reason," Alayna's voice was cautioning.

Philip nodded agreement. "I know."

"It could be for murder for all we know," she replied.

"Beathan wouldn't do that."

Alayna shook her head. "He is capable of much more than you are willing to admit."

"He's not evil." Philip responded, his voice adamant.

"I did not say he was. But he is much more powerful than he lets on," she retorted. Alayna had met Beathan only once more after the events of last winter when his path had crossed with theirs while they were wandering. Philip ignored the underlying warning in her voice.

Alayna pressed on. "I know the past half year has been difficult for you. Adjusting to a new life, to James' murder. I know that somehow you consider Beathan the only partner you have left."

"You're my partner now," Philip whispered, his voice full of love.

Alayna took his face between her cool hands and gazed straight into his eyes for a long, searching moment. Finally, she smiled in wan resignation.

"But you're still going to try and rescue him, aren't you? It's why he sent you this message through his friend and through me. And it's what you're going to try and do. Am I right?" Her voice was tired as if she already knew the answer.

Philip kept a resolute silence. He did not need to tell her what she already knew.

CHAPTER FIVE

The wagon rattled over stone streets for some time and then came to an abrupt halt. They were in a city somewhere. They couldn't be far enough south to have reached St. Thomas's yet, could they? No. No chance. Besides, from what he had heard, the prison was isolated and wouldn't be surrounded by streets. The fake monastery over top of the vault of prison cells was just a façade to fool the unsuspecting. Anyone who looked would just see an old monastery on a rocky shoreline. They would never expect the ulterior motives of the Guild, which had burrowed into the rock beneath the structure to create a web of interconnecting tunnels and caverns and what was likely the most inescapable prison in the world.

Uncertainty, then regret filled him. He should never have convinced Azir to try and contact Alayna. Even if Philip understood what had happened to him and came to help, he was likely to end up beside Beathan in a cell instead of freeing them. It was foolish to involve a friend in his troubles. Beathan made a sour face in frustration at his decision to do so. It had been a moment of weakness. A true trickster got himself out of his own scrapes and didn't rely on the aid of others.

He needed to escape, on his own, and spare Philip the danger of coming to rescue him. He glanced over at his fellow captive. The Elfas was slumped to the side, more listless than unconscious.

"Azir," he whispered as forcefully as he could while still remaining relatively quiet. "Azir! We're stopping."

No response from the dark-featured Elfas. His eyes were open but he was staring before him in a glazed fashion. The face that could be quite charming when cognizant took on a broody look when he was not fully aware of his surroundings. Beathan wasn't sure what was wrong with the Elfas.

Beathan heard soft conversation from outside and then the rattle of keys from his captors as they opened the back doors of the wagon. Quickly, he slumped to the side and let himself hang awkwardly from the wall, allowing his shoulders to wrench uncomfortably. He closed his eyes.

The smell of leather boots and clean cloth filled his nostrils, as well as a vaguely spicy scent—likely some combination of herbs to keep away creatures, such as vampires and werewolves. There was no denying that Collectors were smart. They used every advantage they could and were as prepared as possible.

Beathan kept his eyes shut and his body hanging limp, hoping they would think he was unconscious. It appeared to be working as he felt the Collector fit keys to his manacles and release him to slump to the floor. As he felt the Collector turn away to do the same for Azir, Beathan tapped into his speed through the amplifying bracelet and burst out of the wagon to the milky darkness of a starry night. He had wanted to try and involve Azir in the escape.

As odd and contrary as the Elfas could be at times, Beathan loathed to leave anyone in the clutches of the Guild. And the Elfas had contacted Alayna for him. Even if Beathan now wished he had left his friends out of this mess, either way it showed Azir was willing to work with him. But the Elfas was practically comatose and if Beathan had realized one thing, it was that if you were caught, you escaped when you saw an opportunity. Breakdowns in your captors and chances to regain freedom couldn't always be planned. You had to jump to take your opportunities when they presented.

And so Beathan landed in the street of a city that smelled of refuse and of smoke from factories mixed with the salty tang of a harbor. Liverpool? It did have the scent of that overcrowded environment, but Beathan couldn't be sure, as it had been some years since he had passed that way. His momentary relief and exhilaration at the potential escape collapsed as he saw twenty Collectors arrayed around him.

"You didn't think I was that much of an imbecile, did you? I notified the outpost here in the city to supply us with an entire cohort of my comrades to ensure you make it to the ship suitably bound—and hopefully chastised." The Collector lugging Azir's comatose body taunted him with a self-satisfied smile.

"A lad can dream now, can't he?" Beathan responded with a cocked grin and as much aplomb as possible. He had always relied upon his quick wits to get him out of trouble, and when that wasn't possible, at least his wits deprived the enemy of enjoying the last indignation they sought to inflict on him—his humiliation. After all, he did have a reputation to keep.

"Take him," the Collector behind him commanded.

Beathan flourished a bow to his opponents and mentally embraced the fight to come. He didn't stand a chance.

He'd known it from the start. Even someone as crafty as he couldn't best twenty Collectors—they were too well trained and prepared. Nevertheless, he kicked and hit, he danced one way and then the other in a flash of speed from his amplified bracelet but it was all for naught as they encircled him and tightened formation like a constrictor suffocating its prey. They laid hands on him and overwhelmed him, restraining his arms and legs. So he bit instead. Beathan felt a savage satisfaction as he tasted blood and then felt the stinging, stunning blow of a fist in his face. He laughed anyway. They could hold him and bruise his body but they could never break his spirit.

Then came the ropes. He was hogtied tightly enough to ensure that he would not escape again. Besides, in addition to this fight, he was exhausted from days of captivity without food. He had no real strength left. It was up to Philip now. As much as Beathan now hoped he wouldn't, he knew his one-time Collector friend would indeed come. It was in Philip's nature to try to save and protect people.

"Load them onto the ship," the Collector in charge ordered to his underlings. The two captives were picked up and hauled manually to the harbor. Beathan's limbs screamed in protest from being carried while tied in such a fashion.

He turned to look at the listless Azir. "Looks like it's a sea journey for us after all, Elfas."

Azir groaned and then stuck his tongue out oddly before clamping his jaws down again. He looked like he might be hallucinating.

"It's up to you now, Philip." Beathan whispered to himself. He was not likely to find himself untied again during the journey to St. Thomas's so escape was now out of the question—that chance had flown. Everything now depended on Philip.

CHAPTER SIX

They departed Trondheim on the first ship headed south. A fast ship—a Clipper, a type of ship often used by merchants—for which Philip was glad. The sooner they could return to England, the sooner they could free Beathan.

Captained by a man named Wilfred Wake, the Clipper, would be their home for the next days, until they made port in Liverpool. From there, Philip and Alayna would need to find passage on another ship to make the journey down to the far southern coast of England.

"Steady she is, my gal, Rán," captain Wilf said, rubbing a hand possessively along the handrail on his ship. "You'll not find a better ship on the seas." Philip didn't doubt that the clipper was a good vessel, but he had heard just about every captain of every ship on which he'd set foot make the same statement. Come to think of it, James had spoken similarly of their old ship, the Salt-Spray, during the years his old partner had captained it.

"I'm sure it will suffice," Philip responded politely.

"That it will, lad, that it will." The captain scratched his balding head and then rubbed a hand through his close-cropped, white beard.

A strange looking fellow. Not in general, but odd for a sea captain. Philip couldn't remember the last time he had seen a skinny sea captain. Girth seemed to come with the territory of commanding a ship. Yet Captain Wilf—or 'Captain Wolf' as Philip would overhear the sailors calling him when he was out of earshot—was lean as a rail. He also seemed to live up to his nickname, barking stern orders as he peered shrewdly over the ocean and his deck from behind the wheel of his ship.

Philip shook the captain's hand and thanked him again for agreeing to grant them passage. The old captain just grunted and muttered that there wasn't much to thank him for seeing as how they were damn well going to pay for their passage. He stared fiercely into Philip's eyes for a moment after saying so, as if daring him to say otherwise. Philip imagined that all sorts of rough types might try to scavenge a free ride or duck out before paying upon arrival. Philip held the captain's gaze unconcernedly, until surprisingly, it was the captain who broke eye contact first, looking away, his posture reflecting discomfort. The captain covered it with a cough, but Philip could tell that he wasn't accustomed to being bested in a staring match.

Odd interaction, Philip thought as he went to find Alayna. He had never been a particularly formidable man in appearance. All the danger Philip possessed was hidden deep within his deceptively thin, ordinary frame. Strange that he should have caused such a reaction in the captain.

He found Alayna with the rest of their few possessions in the single, tiny cabin reserved for passengers. One bunk that could hardly fit a single person would have to do for both of them at night. A chair was bolted to the floor in the corner, and that was the extent of the furniture. Rough seas could cause the worst of damage, even on the interior of a ship, and the North Atlantic was far from a calm stretch of ocean.

Wilfred Wake was probably a frugal and practical man, as most sea captains were. He wouldn't waste time or money on fixing broken frivolities. Philip had a feeling that everything other than the tiny bunk was likely seen just so in the captain's eyes.

Alayna was catnapping on the bunk with a cloak pulled over her like a blanket, one leg stretched out from underneath it to hang off the bed. She could find a moment to sleep even in the midst of a storm. He didn't know how she did it. He had only left her a few minutes ago to acquaint himself with the captain, yet here she was managing to make it appear as if this tiny room was the most comfortable she had ever occupied. She owned the space with her personality as if it really belonged to her.

Alayna awoke with a lethargic smile as if she had really been awakening from a deep sleep, not a five-minute snatch of shut-eye. She stretched her arms above her head, which happened to allow the cloak to slip to the floor revealing her slender curved body.

"Care to join me?" she asked in her most sultry, seductive voice. She let out a wicked giggle at what must have been a look of longing on Philip's face and then switched to a more normal tone.

"Come here, my love," It was a quiet, affectionate command and Philip obeyed.

They spent an hour in the luxury of each other's arms, a slow hurricane of heated limbs and hot breath, until they finally experienced the ecstasy of completion. They simply lay together then, on the narrow bunk, the room scattered with their clothes as if a whirlwind had blown through it. Philip closed his eyes and felt the motion of the ship, up, down, up, down, slowly but steadily, as it beat its way up the front of a swell and down its face on the other side.

He gradually drifted off amidst the motion of the sea, the faint smell of heather in Alayna's hair mixing with the tang of the ocean air. He didn't know how long he slept but he was awakened with an elbow to his gut.

He grunted and tried to give the wriggling Alayna some room to maneuver on the tiny bed. She laughed her apologies and continued to squirm until she had worked her way around and was now face to face with him instead of back to front. She looked at him for a long moment and Philip thought she was about to say something, but instead she just kissed him deliberately and then closed her eyes again as if to fall back asleep.

"All that writhing for a simple position change?" Philip joked.

"Writhing!" Alayna exclaimed in mock indignation.

"Or should I say wriggling?" Philip asked. "Well, if you wanted to wriggle...." He did not finish his sentence but instead began to tickle her, enjoying her bubbling screams. It was only for a moment, and then he stopped and held her laughing body close to his again.

"You're an oaf! Now I'll never fall back asleep," She mumbled into his chest, conveniently forgetting the elbow she had planted in his stomach a few moments earlier. But Philip could tell she wasn't angry, in fact, she seemed very comfortable.

She turned her face up to look at his again, her pale, elegant features filling his vision the way her presence had come to fill his life.

"Has it ever been done before?" She asked in a serious voice.

"What's that, my love?"

"What it is we are going to do. Has it ever been accomplished?"

Comprehension lit in Philip's mind as their conversation spun back towards important matters. He rued the disappearance of the pleasant time they had spent relaxing in each other's company.

"I do not know whether it has ever been accomplished, Alayna. Even if someone did manage to break into St. Thomas's and free creatures at some point in the past, it is the sort of information the Guild would keep a closely guarded secret, and therefore we are not likely to know."

Philip sighed as he thought of the immensity of their task. They were both aware that to free Beathan almost certainly meant breaking into the Guild's prison stronghold and trying to loose the half-breed in the process.

He continued. "However, if I had to guess, I would bet that it had never been done. We seek to do what others have deemed impossible."

Alayna nodded her head in acceptance. "How will we do it?"

"I have no idea," Philip groaned as he was forced to admit that fact, and then sat up, breaking their embrace in the frustration of not having the answer they needed. He swung his legs off the bed so that his bare feet rested on the rough wooden floor.

Alayna sat up with him and put a comforting hand on his shoulder. She didn't voice any empty platitudes to try and make him feel better. They both knew the immensity of the task ahead of them. Breaking into St. Thomas's was more likely to end in their demise—or worse their capture—as it was to yield a victory. Alayna just let her presence comfort him in silence.

They sat for a moment until Alayna put one hand to her head and squinted in what appeared to be confusion. Terror thundered through Philip, as he feared she was about to undergo the torture she had experienced near the wharf in Trondheim again. But she dropped her hand quickly and shook her head in answer to his unspoken question. Relief replaced most of his anxiety, but a kernel of worry remained.

"What is it, Alayna? Is it the pain again?"

"It's nothing really. There's no pain. It just feels like... it feels as if there's a residue left on my mind from the last painful contact. It doesn't hurt, but it feels... soiled. Like an oil slick on water. The two liquids can touch and move as one but they don't really mix."

"And this has never happened before?" Philip questioned. He hated not knowing what was happening. In his previous profession as a Collector, he had always sought to his utmost to understand every aspect of every job that he had ever taken. Knowledge gave a person the advantage. Right now he felt powerless.

"Never," Alayna responded. "Not only is this dirty feeling new when connecting with the mind of one of my kind, but I have also never felt any prolonged connection to the mind after they have ended the contact. It's as if I can still feel whoever's consciousness it was, hovering just around a corner. It's strange."

Philip pursed his lips as he thought. New things were often bad things. Not always, but in the realm of the supernatural, novelty often came with a price.

"Do you know what it means, love?" He clasped her hand as he asked.

Alayna just shook her head.

———

THE VOYAGE from Trondheim to Liverpool shouldn't have taken more than a few days, but a late summer squall arose, slowing their passage. On the first day Philip and Alayna dressed and left the cabin. Philip pulled on his battered, old breeches and the faded tunic, unlaced at the throat. The sleeves were torn off and he liked them that way. "His boots clumped loudly on the wood of the deck while Alayna's soft leather boots whispered beside him."

His boots clumped loudly on the wood of the deck while Alayna's soft leather boots whispered beside him.

They moved up on deck to grab some fresh air and stood along the rail watching the sailors work as the ocean passed by around them. Philip enjoyed the crisp cold quality of the air. It was not exactly uncommon for it to be cold, even in late summer. This far north, autumn and subsequently winter came much sooner than in lands to the south. The bite of winter was harsh in the northern regions of the world.

The second day of the voyage turned even colder. Night had brought a frost and light snowflakes began to drift down among the masts and rigging. Not enough to stick, the flakes melted as soon as they touched a warm body, but a few did manage to cluster into small piles in more shadowy corners of the ship's deck.

Philip felt a thrill of joy at watching the first snow of the year. With a sense of caution, he embraced the excitement, the energy of the cold and snowfall. This wasn't his human side. For many years, he had enjoyed snow no more and no less than any average person. But this wholehearted, and almost otherworldly, feeling of elation at the year's first snow originated in a different part of his blood altogether. It was the troll blood flowing through his veins, his untamed side that loved the ice and cold, the crispness of the air and the scent of a kill kept clean and fresh by the snow.

He shrugged his shoulders uncomfortably. He had come to grips with the truth that he was a hybrid, no longer completely human. He had accepted it and even relished in it at times.

But at moments like this when he felt anticipation and genuine pleasure at something he had not even known he liked, he felt the most unsure of the wildness within him. What if one day it consumed him altogether and he found himself more beast than man?

He shook his head, determination stiffening his frame. No. That day would never happen. He thought of the ill-advised encounter with the troll from a few days gone, and the list of aggressive behavior Alayna had ticked off at their camp. He couldn't deny he was changing, adapting, little by little to his new self. He must make certain that by accepting and embracing his hybrid nature he would not end up more monster than man.

Alayna crept up and hugged him from behind and his worries ebbed immediately. He was not likely to become a monster around her. She was the furthest thing from a monster and by extension she kept him similarly sensitive to the world around him.

Snow had begun to fall in earnest while he had been pondering his future, and the sailors grumbled and cursed the sea gods for the misfortune of having to tie ropes and man the rigging with stiff fingers and numb feet.

"You're making them nervous, love." Alayna's comment surprised him enough to shake him out of the contemplative mood in which he'd been.

"What?" He crinkled his eyebrows in confusion.

"I said you are making the crew nervous." She teased him by saying the words slowly and deliberately, one at a time.

"I heard what you said, Alayna. But what do you mean?"

Alayna pointedly wrapped her arms around herself and shivered. At some point she must have gone back into the cabin and put on her cloak.

"I mean, it's been snowing for hours now and most people's fingers and hands are growing numb. The crew have all donned their sea coats long since. Yet, here you stand, sleeveless, and seemingly untouched by the cold."

She paused and put her hands up in a conciliatory gesture. "I'm not saying you have to do something about it, make them nervous for all I care. I do love you when you're looking your most feral." She smiled mischievously, "But you are the one who tends to want to avoid any unwanted notice. And you are definitely attracting attention right now."

Feral? Philip didn't think he gave off that vibe. But, she was right. Philip glanced around and saw the crewmembers stealing uncomfortable sidelong glances at him. Philip wasn't displaying any sort of crazy supernatural ability. Yet, staying hidden and safe from the Guild meant protecting your identity. Little clues such as a person not showing a hint of cold or goose bumps in the frigid snowy air could be enough to make people wonder.

He nodded. "Alright, you're correct, Alayna. I'll deal with it."

The trouble was, he really didn't get cold any more. At least, not in the way a man did. He didn't have a cloak or a coat with him. The best course of action was probably to try and buy one off the crew or maybe the captain. Yes, the captain was the most likely to have a spare sea coat to sell.

Philip left Alayna leaning over the rail, her golden red hair spilling out from under her dark hood as she peered down in the grey-blue waters of the North Atlantic sweeping by beneath them. He walked up to the captain's deck where Wilf was holding the tiller of his ship nonchalantly. But Philip could see that it was a practiced complacence. The man was ready for anything the sea could throw at him—he just acted like he wasn't.

The ship rocked under Philip's feet as he made his way up to the captain. The sea had grown rough with the squall. The snow was changing to sleet and there was a coat of frost on parts of the deck so Philip picked his steps carefully.

"Captain." Philip inclined his head.

"Philip." The captain responded.

Philip cut to the point. He might banter with Alayna—the person with whom he was the most intimate—but with others, strangers in particular, Philip was not really a man of many words. He spoke simply, in accordance with the way he looked, and didn't waste his breath.

"I seem to find myself unprepared," he lied. "I have no coat and was not expecting the weather to break before the heart of autumn."

"What does that have to do with me, lad?" The reed-thin, grizzled sea captain asked, his nonchalant appearance belied by the way his eyes darted to and fro across his deck observing the activity of his ship and crew.

47

"I thought perhaps you might have a spare coat." Philip saw Wilf's face darken briefly before Philip added, "to purchase. A spare coat for purchase. I will pay well."

Wilf's face brightened. "Well, I just might have one at that. Thorgen!" He bellowed to his first mate and watched as the heavy bodied Norwegian made his way to the captain's deck on spritely sea legs that belied his girth. Thorgen was more like what Philip was accustomed to seeing in a captain. Wide of body and of face, he had a thick full beard that was going grey and had never been cut. The hair spread out magnificently over his chest. He had a deep voice to suit.

"Aye, Cap'n."

"Take the tiller, Thorgen, until I return." Captain Wilfred Wake handed over the tiller of his ship to the capable first mate and led Philip down the steps towards the deck and then into the aft cabin to the captain's quarters. Philip followed diligently.

"You've got the legs of a man who's spent time at sea, Philip," the captain said observantly. "Perhaps not recently, but I've seen your sea legs return to you over the past days.

"You are correct, Captain. I was co-owner of a vessel for some years, sailing back and forth from Britain to the Americas. Alas, the ship was lost in a storm and I am now on more difficult times."

The lie sprang easily to his lips. His ship hadn't been lost in a storm at all. It had been damaged in Astori's attack—the attack in which James had perished. Philip felt a pang of guilt at how he had abandoned, not just his ship, but also his dead friend to the care of others.

He hoped the Guild had caught wind of what had happened in time to capture the creatures that had been loosed in New York City and also to transport his partner James' body back across the Atlantic to his family.

The captain nodded acceptingly as he rummaged through a storage locker in his room. Finally, he grabbed something and yanked it out.

"Ha! Here it is." He held an old, navy-blue pea coat with buttons up one of the sides and a thick collar that could be turned up against a stormy wind to keep a man warm.

"That looks fine to me." Philip said. The coat would do. It didn't have to be the best coat on the planet, it just had to fool the crew and appease the standards of common practice in order to stop drawing attention to himself.

Wilf's face took on a sly look and Philip saw why they called him 'wolf'. It had to do with more than just the similarity with his name.

"I'll give it to you if you triple your passage fee. Transport for you and your lady plus this coat for triple what we said initially," he stated boldly, thrusting his bristly white chin at Philip.

"Double," Philip countered.

Wilfred Wake paused a moment as if gauging his passenger's level of desperation.

Philip interrupted his pondering. "You'll not get a penny more than double. If you won't sell for that price, I'll just spend the whole voyage in the relative warmth of my cabin and you'll have missed out on an excellent opportunity to make a profit. I know this isn't the only spare coat you have buried somewhere in storage."

Wilf grunted his assent and shook hands with Philip. "Double then. See that you pay up when we reach port. I'll not be taken, no I won't!"

"Of course, Captain, you'll have the extra money when we reach Liverpool. You have my word."

Transaction done, they left the cabin and Philip slid his arms through the old coat sleeves. It was old and smelled of pipe smoke and dried salt, but it fit perfectly. He and the old captain were similar in height and build. They had their leanness in common.

Philip left the coat unbuttoned as he went back on deck. He was not above bowing to societal convention in order to hide his true nature—he had bought the coat to blend in with the crew—but he wasn't about to button up the coat and suffer unnecessary sweltering heat. His body ran hotter than most these days, courtesy of his trollish heritage, and if sleeves were annoyance enough, imagine what a winter coat would feel like.

He made his way back to Alayna and they stood together, backs against the rail, observing the ship's activity. The sailors were busy, as usual, moving quickly to the barked orders of Thorgen.

"There, much better," Alayna winked at him. "You blend right in now. Well, all but your eyes, of course."

"My eyes?"

"Yes, they have a decidedly untamed look to them. Enough that a simple coat can't cover it up." She smiled fondly, gazing into what were apparently his savage eyes. "Be easy love, there is nothing to be done about it. It's impossible to completely hide who we truly are. Inevitably signs remain of our real identities."

The wind gusted and blew her hair for an instant, revealing her beautifully tipped ears as if to punctuate he statement. Then the wind fell and her hair settled, hiding them again. She pulled her cloak around her, tightening the hood to her head slightly, which prevented the wind from gathering it again.

It was true. They were who they were. The world might revile them if they knew, but you could only hide so much.

———

THE SIXTH DAY of their weather-slowed journey proved to be their final. They had sailed along the north and then west coast of Scotland, down through the strait between Britain and Ireland until they arrived in the comparatively calm Irish Sea.

Being so close to Ireland reminded Philip of Beathan. On their journey across the Atlantic towards the Nordic countries some months ago, Philip and Alayna's path had taken them briefly through Ireland. As fortune would have it, the inn at which they stayed was also housing the roguish Irish half-breed. The three of them had enjoyed each other's company and the half gypsy, half fairy, had regaled them with tales of his rapscallion exploits that had them in fits of laughter.

Philip later realized it was a testament to how much he'd changed that he was able to listen to Beathan recount his various acts of thievery with relatively little judgment. The Collector he had been would have found himself hard pressed not to judge the fairy for stealing from innocent folk. But the new him, the Philip that was coming to terms with his own wild nature, understood that sometimes it was easier to give in to one's nature than to fight it.

Besides, more often than not, Beathan would return the trinket he had stolen in some comical fashion that made the whole encounter more of a joke, than a violation of property. Philip could accept that sort of mischief. After all, the fairy was his friend, had risked his life with Philip to stop Astori and save Alayna. There were worse things in life than a person with light fingers. He grinned, reflecting on the last encounter with his friend, until his mirth was stifled by the realization of the difficult and dangerous task ahead of them.

Alayna seemed to read his mind. "We'll make it happen. Somehow, we will." They stood together in the prow of the ship. Philip, with his coat unbuttoned, his hands in his pockets, and his feet planted firmly apart for stabilization. Alayna seemed impervious to the sea swells. She paid no attention to how one was supposed to walk or stand on a ship, yet she was nimble and graceful in only the way one of the Elfas could be. She never for a moment looked off balance.

"Do you have any ideas about how we'll do it?" She asked tentatively.

"Nothing substantial yet," he replied. He wished he had a plan ready, but there were just the rumblings of an idea, not fully formed yet, not ready for discussion. He needed to think more.

Alayna was in an inquisitive mood. "What do you suppose the Guild thinks of you? What is your standing with them?"

"I am probably presumed dead," Philip said matter-of-factly. "The extent of the wounds on the body of James and the crew, the damaged ship, and the lone return of my apprentice, Stephen, to England, will have given evidence of the difficulties we faced last winter."

He paused, thinking about all the people who must have been terrorized by a whole cargo of supernatural killers released on New York by Astori. It had all been part of the mad magician's plot to strengthen his powers by magically binding those creatures to himself and gaining health and youth from the destruction the creatures caused as they used their own supernatural abilities.

"Yes, that's right, they would know of James' death," Alayna said.

"Not just his," Philip responded, "there were a number of Guild members in New York who were killed by Astori. A catastrophe for the Guild. An entire shipload of creatures freed, and a handful of members dead in the space of a day. When I didn't return, they likely assumed me dead in a gutter after trying to recapture the prisoners. Dead or eaten."

"Eaten." Alayna shuddered compulsively.

"There are many creatures who wouldn't think twice about consuming a man. I told you of the Wendigo, did I not?" She nodded her assent. "And that's not even mentioning the veritable slew of vampires I've hunted over the years," he finished.

Alayna thought for a moment before speaking. "I am thankful I became what I am, one of the Alderfolk, instead of something monstrous."

"You were lucky," Philip conceded. Then on impulse he asked a question he hadn't asked before, one he was slightly frightened to ask because there was no recourse either way. "Do you ever miss being human, Miss Oakdale?"

He tried to frame the question as a joke so as to conceal his fear about her response. She wasn't human any longer and that was his fault. If he had not courted her, Astori would likely never have even known of her existence and would therefore not have used her in his experiment—his attempt to recreate the Great Transformation.

She eyed Philip for a moment. "I haven't been 'Miss Oakdale' for quite some time now. And I will never be again. My humanity is fading like a dream from some distant night." Alayna trailed off thoughtfully, with a melancholy look. Philip's gut twisted. She did miss being human and it was entirely his fault.

Always intuitive, she sensed his discomfort and put a hand on his cheek. She deliberately brightened her expression. "We are together. We live a good life. The days when I miss it, I miss the memory of normality more than anything else, the way you miss something from your childhood, even though you know it would not be anywhere near as good now as your memory has created it to be."

Philip smiled. She was good at soothing his worries. And he could tell she wasn't lying. They were happy together. He knew that much was true.

Alayna seemed determined to lighten the mood. "What would you have done if I had turned into a vampire instead of an Elfas?" She asked playfully.

"I'd have staked you." Philip kept his face straight as he said it.

Alayna stared at him in horror until she saw the slow wink he gave her.

"You're horrible!" Alayna giggled and slapped his shoulders in exasperation with the back of her knuckles. A playful tap, not genuine annoyance.

Philip chuckled as she stared out to sea primly, trying to ignore the fact that he had tricked her. His laughter died on his lips though, as he contemplated his statement. He was teasing, but the terrible reality was that somewhere deep down there was a kernel of truth.

If Alayna had turned into something terribly dangerous and volatile, he would have at least considered putting her down gently for a split second. For her own good. She wasn't the type of person who could have lived with herself as a deadly monster. He shuddered at the thought of killing Alayna. She was his life now. He was changed, a different man. Back then the idea of killing her would have been brutal but he would have considered it. Now, the idea of doing so was more reprehensible than anything he could contemplate. He'd sooner tear off his arm or end his own life as deliberately injure her.

———

THE LAST DAY of the voyage passed uneventfully. As they neared Liverpool they began to see an increase of ships and vessels sailing in opposite directions and also alongside them. Liverpool was a hub of English trade. Merchant vessels made port here, both as a final destination for their goods and also as a stopping point of a much longer journey.

Captain Wilfred Wake was making port here for a number of days. His ship and crew, he told Alayna and Philip, had been sailing hard for quite some time now, long before they had reached Trondheim.

They sailed into the immense harbor and dropped anchor. The captain arranged a skiff to take them ashore with him. He had business to attend to before he could return to ship, pay his men, and give them shore leave.

"Liverpool's ugly as they come. It smells like piss and chamber pots," Wilfred Wake proclaimed cheerfully, "but it's a hell of a city to make a profit." He rubbed his hands together almost unconsciously as he thought about his business. Philip had paid him the rest of the fare promised in exchange for the coat upon their arrival and the man's eyes had lit up at the money like a child's for toys or sweets.

Philip just didn't get it. Even as a Collector when he had been clinging to his human side, money had never been important to him. Doing a job and doing it well. Being of use to the world. That was what had occupied his thoughts.

He nodded politely, not wanting to dispute the captain's emphasis on money and start an argument just when they were about to depart one another's company. Alayna shook Wilf's hand delicately with her thin fingers and surprisingly, the captain blushed at her touch. He held her hand for a moment longer and glanced at Philip. His blush turned to a gulp and he quickly released Alayna's hand. Something in Philip's eyes had unsettled him, but what it was, Philip had no idea.

"M'lady, Philip, was a pleasure doing business with you." The captain spared one more look at Philip before he hurried away muttering about his pressing business.

Alayna scolded Philip with a glance and said, "There was no need for that look, Philip."

He shrugged and widened his eyes innocently. He wasn't even sure what he had done. Maybe his eyes did unsettle people with their wildness. He said as much to Alayna and she snorted a laugh.

"Love, I don't think it was your wild nature scaring him off. This time, I'm pretty sure it was just the look in the eyes of a jealous man."

Philip shook his head at her teasing but took it in good-natured silence. He didn't think of himself as particularly jealous. He certainly hadn't been trying to be jealous with the captain. But if a man were to be jealous over anyone, it would be someone like Alayna.

They walked in the opposite direction from Wilfred Wake, meandering their way through the crowd of people at the harbor for their daily business. Suddenly, a familiar face stood out in the crowd. Philip would recognize that face anywhere. The boy was leaner, taller than he had been half a year gone when Philip had last seen him, but there was no denying the fact that it was his old apprentice, Stephen.

CHAPTER SEVEN

The sun was sinking as they left the port. They followed Stephen for a few city blocks, tailing him through the milling throngs of people. The boy surefootedly danced his way in and around carts and between merchants, who were in heated debates with one another over the worth of their goods. Philip and Alayna kept their distance, not wanting to be seen prematurely. Philip wanted to speak with the boy, but he wanted to do so in quiet, away from the prying eyes and ears of the city. Stephen glanced about and behind him every so often and Philip noticed that the lad seemed to have changed in more ways than just his added height. He was more cautious, doubling back every now and again, in a manner Philip was almost certain was unnecessary in order to reach his desired destination.

After a number of blocks of careful meanderings, Stephen finally ducked into a quieter side alley. The street was narrow and had strings of washed clothes hanging between windows to dry. A few piles of offal, from what had to be emptied chamber pots, decorated the gutters and emitted a putrid stink that permeated the air all around them.

Just as Philip and Alayna entered the alleyway behind the boy, Stephen whirled, a tiny knife in his hand, and declared fiercely, "Don't come any closer. I'm armed and you'll deserve what you get!" He waved his knife in the air menacingly.

"Easy lad, we mean you no harm," Philip took a few cautious steps forward through the shadows.

"I know you've been following me," Stephen's voice warbled and cracked under the pressure of the situation. "I mean it, don't come a step closer!"

"Stephen, relax, we aren't here to hurt you." Philip continued forward slowly, motioning Alayna to stay behind him just in case.

As Philip stepped out of the shadows a patch of light illuminated his features. The boy's jaw dropped in astonishment and it was a moment before he recovered from the shock.

"Master Philip, you're alive!" He gasped. "It can't be! I thought for certain you were dead last winter when you didn't return to the ship. Although, I began to hope maybe you weren't last week when..." Stephen seemed to shake his mind clear and stopped babbling.

"Sir, why are you here?"

"It's not sir or master any longer lad, just Philip. You are not my apprentice anymore." He eased up to the boy and clapped him on the shoulder in friendship, ignoring the question for now. "Sorry to scare you, I just didn't want our reunion to be public."

"I wasn't frightened," Stephen denied stoutly, although the way his eyes flicked nervously around the alley said otherwise.

"Of course not lad, I didn't mean it that way. I just meant we surprised you, that's all." He protected the boy's fragile self-esteem as best he could. Philip introduced Alayna. "This is Alayna, the woman I told you about last winter before we parted ways."

"Pleased to meet you, Stephen, Philip has spoken highly of you during these last months." Alayna knew how to flatter a person without directly lying. Philip had indeed said one or two good things about the boy to her when they had spoken of the events in New York, but it wasn't as if they'd had many conversations about Stephen.

Yet from the way she spoke, you would think it was all they talked about in their free time. Of which they had an excessive amount, Philip realized with a grin. Without professions any more, time was in ample supply. They lived off the land and went where they pleased, when they pleased.

Stephen flushed and his back straightened under the compliment. Philip fought back a smile as he watched. "Life must be a bit rough around here for you to be so jumpy, eh lad?" Philip prodded for some answers.

"You don't know the half of it," the boy's maturing voice couldn't decide on a pitch as he responded. "Ever since the events of last winter, when… well, you know what it was that happened." Stephen paused and rolled his shoulders uncomfortably before continuing.

"Go on," Alayna encouraged gently.

"Well, after last winter, what with all the dead members and what happened in the city afterwards, with all those creatures angry and loose, the Guild began pressing harder. The last six months or so we've had orders to pick up anything nonhuman, dangerous or not, doesn't matter." Stephen spoke rapidly as if his thoughts scampered over each other the way a boy's mind sometimes did.

Philip felt a pang of guilt for leaving New York in such circumstances after killing Astori. He could have stayed and tried to recapture the prisoners, but instead he had left a cargo hold full of vampires, werewolves, witches and more, loose on an unsuspecting city. The price of his disappearance.

Stephen was still talking as Philip split his focus between listening and thinking. The boy's voice gained speed and anxiety. "Well, the other side —those we hunt—didn't take too kindly to the campaign to put them all away. They fought back. Guild members have been going missing and dying regularly, and in response, the Guild pushes harder to nab more beasties and it's a vicious cycle. I thought you were coming to grab me, that maybe you weren't human, you know?" He finished in a small voice, as he seemed to realize he had just implicitly admitted to the fear he had so adamantly denied earlier.

To recover his pride, the boy grabbed the hilt of the knife that he had just replaced in its sheath and said, "But I wasn't about to go without a fight!"

"No doubt, Stephen, you would have acquitted yourself just fine," Philip murmured soothingly even though he was fairly sure the boy would have been dead in a heartbeat. He was too young for that sort of fight. Apprentices were not trained by the Guild in combat and weaponry until fifteen at the earliest, more often sixteen years of age. Stephen couldn't be more than thirteen now, still young enough to only be used as a runner and for menial tasks.

The boy's comments unsettled Philip. It sounded almost like the Guild and the supernatural realm were in an outright war. That hadn't happened for decades. It hadn't been like that since the mysterious Great Transformation, when overnight the supernatural realm of creatures had multiplied exponentially and began wreaking havoc on the human realm. The Great Transformation had necessitated a full-scale mobilization by the Guild in order to combat the dangerous myths and legends that were born into the world in such quick and sudden succession.

Alayna spoke then, questioning the boy gently. "You said you assumed Philip was dead?" It matched their guesses on what the Guild assumed about Philip.

The boy nodded. "I overheard a conversation between a couple of members a few months back. They said Philip couldn't have taken on the whole cargo load of freed prisoners alone. They figured he'd died in the attempt. I reckoned the same back then when you didn't show up the next day." He directed this last comment at Philip.

"But earlier you said you weren't sure anymore. What changed?" Alayna was insightful. She had picked up on an important piece of information in the midst of the boy's initial rush of babbling surprise.

Stephen flicked an uncertain glance at Philip. "Well, I saw *him*. The one you were with last winter, Sir."

"Who?" Philip prodded wanting the boy to answer without any preconceptions.

"The gypsy half-breed." Stephen answered. "'Bout a week gone now I was cleaning the hold on one of the Guild ships when I saw them drag him in unconscious and bound. He looked pretty battered, as if he'd put up quite a fight."

Philip winced as he thought of free spirited Beathan chained and shackled in a prison transport ship. Sometimes it was astounding to him to think back to those times a half year gone, when as a Collector, he had simply followed orders. He would have done the same thing to Beathan then.

In fact, he had tried, but the wily hybrid fairy had eluded him. The one positive thing to take from Stephen's information was the knowledge that Beathan was ahead of them in transport. That meant Philip and Alayna wouldn't have to worry about trying to ascertain when the fairy reached St. Thomas's, because he would almost certainly arrive there ahead of them. They could focus on trying to hatch a plan to save him.

Stephen wasn't done speaking. "I figured if *he* was still alive, then maybe you were too, Sir. I wasn't too hopeful, but even a little bit of hope is better than nothing."

"Was he captured alone?" Alayna, once again, asked the question that Philip should have been asking instead of reminiscing about times past.

"No, he was with another prisoner, a man, or creature, I don't know. Matter of fact, his fellow prisoner looked a lot like you, Miss Alayna. 'Cept he had darker hair and eyes. But his features were thin like yours and his ears..." The boy trailed off and his eyes widened as he realized what he was implying by drawing a connection between Alayna and a Guild captive. He glanced at Philip nervously.

Philip reassured his old apprentice with a smile and a hand on his back. "It's alright lad, she's not dangerous. No need to worry." Alayna smiled her reassurance, as well, and the boy seemed to relax again, trusting them.

"So are you coming back to the Guild then, Sir?" Stephen asked tentatively. His young face fell at Philip's response.

"No, lad, that part of my life is over now. For a number of reasons. Reasons I can't fully explain to you here and now."

Philip had been a Collector for most of his life. But for most of his life he had fought his wild heritage, the troll blood that mixed and flowed alongside his human blood. To go back to hunting supernatural creatures on behalf of the Guild seemed hypocritical in the most extreme fashion considering his own supernatural nature. Reaching that conclusion had been a process years in the making, but when it had come, Philip had cut ties with the Guild completely.

On that fateful night after defeating Astori, instead of returning to his former employers, he had run north with Alayna. He had finally accepted himself for what he truly was—a hybrid. He had tapped into his wild nature—a side of himself that had lain dormant for decades—to defeat Astori and save Alayna. It had been necessary, but it had also been the right thing to do. Accepting the truth about himself had allowed him to tap into his abilities to a fuller extent. Where previously he had only been able to use his supernatural strength, due to the repression of his true nature, now Philip could do more. He could heal more quickly and withstand certain magic.

Stephen's face twisted in disappointment, but Philip spoke on, "It's for the best, I believe. Especially now that they're rounding up anything with arms, legs, and magic." The last part Philip spoke with unexpected bitterness. It galled him that his fairy friend was in the clutches of the Guild.

Stephen peered at Philip for a moment. "You're going to rescue him, aren't you, Sir?"

The boy's clarity and perceptiveness caught Philip off guard and he stayed silent, not answering, but Stephen was insistent.

"I can help, Master Philip. I can help you, like old times."

Philip felt the boy's plea tug on his heartstrings. "Imagine I was going to break him free, why would you want to be part of such a dangerous plot?" He looked at the boy seriously, weighing the emotions that played across his old apprentice's face. It was clear the boy had missed him.

The boy opened his mouth to answer but Philip changed his mind and interrupted him. "No, never mind, lad. We'll speak no more of it. There'll be no rescue attempt. As far as you know, we are doing nothing of the kind. I'll not have you involved in anything dangerous. I don't want you running afoul of the Guild. That never turns out well for anyone."

Philip hoped his evasiveness would be enough to put the boy off. He was a smart boy; Philip had always known that about Stephen. Figuring out what they were about without having to be told was proof of his intelligence. But he was also smart enough to realize the truth when he heard it.

He knew, as well as Philip, that a person did not want to end up on the wrong side of the Collectors. It was the same reason Philip had left with Alayna last winter instead of checking in with the Guild. If word had gotten out that he had partnered up with a fairy, was in love with one of the Alderfolk, and worst of all, had the blood of trolls running in his veins making him a hybrid, the Guild would without a doubt have turned on him.

"Twilight is nearly upon us," Alayna murmured, conveniently changing the subject. "We will need someplace to sleep tonight, Philip. Shall we find somewhere to pay for a bed or would you prefer to make our camp outside the city limits?"

Philip wanted nothing more than to get out of this stinking city. He already missed the fresh scent of pines, the smell of smoke from the fire, and meat roasting on a spit. Their finances were depleted and they needed to conserve what little they had for passage south on another ship. Any bed they could afford tonight was bound to be riddled with bedbugs or worse. He pursed his lips thoughtfully, trying to decide what they should do.

Stephen answered for him. "You can stay with me, Sir, Miss Alayna."

Philip shared a questioning glance with Alayna in consideration of the boy's proposal. She shrugged her shoulders almost imperceptibly, as if to ask what they had to lose.

"I don't live in official Guild quarters. I stay with my aunt's cousin—though what that makes her to me I've no idea—and nobody from the Guild needs to know you're there for the night." The boy once again intuited correctly, deducing from their previous conversation that Philip wanted to avoid the notice of the Guild while in Liverpool.

"Alright then, Stephen, lead the way." Philip gestured that they would follow the boy and clasped hands with Alayna as they walked.

The sun had set during their discussion in the alley and the last gasp of the day's light cast lengthy shadows on the city streets. As they walked, Stephen chattered happily. He spoke about his job with the Guild—it sounded almost identical to what he had done for Philip, only he worked at a primary Guild outpost rather than with a partnership on the move—and about his family and his dog.

He must be lonely Philip thought with a sudden rush of sympathy. He wasn't the only one who had lost a friend last winter when James had died. Stephen had lost him too. Only, Stephen had thought Philip was dead also. The boy had lost two friends instead of one. Philip tried to imagine how he would feel if he saw James walking around one day after thinking him dead for six months. Philip imagined he might be similarly giddy.

The day was dying. Dusk grew on the city of Liverpool and the last vestiges of golden light finally disappeared, leaving them walking in lantern-lit darkness.

"It's not much farther now," Stephen proclaimed, turning a corner and marching steadily forward.

As they followed him around the corner, Philip felt a prickling sensation between his shoulder blades and an uneasy tension in the air. They were close to Stephen's home but something unsettled his senses. Long ago as a Collector he had learned to trust his instincts. He put a restraining hand on Stephen's shoulder to stop the boy and freed his other hand from where it had been clasped comfortably with Alayna's warm fingers. He wanted his fighting hands available.

"What is it?" Alayna questioned, putting a hand to the hilt of the knife she wore at her belt.

"Not sure, love, but something tells me we've got company." He pulled them onto a side street. Moving away from the more used thoroughfares might make an attack more likely, but it would also protect innocent strangers who were out in the night. Philip wasn't a Collector anymore but he still felt the same urge to protect those unable to defend themselves. The last thing he wanted was to stir up trouble for the folk in Stephen's neighborhood.

They were now in an empty alley and sure enough the conflict came. A shape dropped effortlessly down from the dark rooftops to land a few yards away from them. A levitation spell was the only thing that could make a person float like that.

Witch.

Philip hoped it wasn't what he thought it might be. His hopes were dashed as the figure stepped out of the shadows and into the light of a lantern. A human face stared malevolently at him, human except for the blue tinge to the skin. It looked the way a body did when it had been too long in the water, and absorbed a bluish cast. There were darker blue veins streaking across the face, as well, to give it a decidedly ghoulish cast. There were not many dangers Philip could think of that were worse to face than a Black Annis—the infamous claw-handed witches.

Legends in England spoke of the Black Annis as if there were only one of them. Stories said that an old hag was the witch who ate children and committed other unspeakable acts of cruelty. Any time a Black Annis was sighted, the people usually attributed it to the same witch, creating the mythology surrounding the name that made Black Annis into a fearsome and singular magical being.

Yet, the truth was simple. The Black Annises were a category of creature, and there were many of them spread around Britain and even elsewhere in the world. They were most commonly found near their sanctuary in the Dane Hills, a system of underground caverns that even the Guild had been loathe to penetrate without good cause, due to the near impossibility of navigating its endless tunnels in the dark. The warrior witches who lived there—the Black Annises—would make short work of any Collectors who ventured into their lair. No, it was best to wait and pick them off in solitary fashion elsewhere in the land.

The Black Annis extended an arm and Philip saw the clawed hand flex and then flick as it prepared to fight and he felt a chill run down his spine. He hadn't felt like this since before the events of last winter. It had been a while since he faced a foe that he truly feared. Even the troll from a week gone was more brutish and bestial than sinister.

"Get behind me," he muttered hoarsely to Alayna and Stephen. They didn't stand a chance against a Black Annis but he might. The clawed witch was part of a race of beings that possessed not only the physical attributes necessary to be a dangerous opponent in combat—their claws each like a small knife blade—but they also were magical in the manner of witches. They fought with spells and claws, with strength and with the mystical mutterings of an ancient and dark magic.

Alayna and Stephen couldn't withstand that power, but Philip's troll blood gave him an advantage they didn't have. He was impervious to most magic. Or at least magic didn't affect him quite as drastically as it did others. His troll characteristics might be able to win this fight for him.

Philip took a step forward to engage the Black Annis when it raised its knife-like fingers for him to stop. He paused.

"We want the boy. You may leave unharmed, Half-breed." The voice sounded like a pestle grinding against a mortar. How had it known he wasn't fully man? Magic. He would do well to remember that the Black Annises possessed unknown quantities of magic. One of the lesser-studied dark creatures by the Guild, not a lot was known about their potential other than that they were vicious and best taken down when the numbers were on your side.

Wait, *we*? The Black Annis had said *we*.

Just then, Philip's expectations of surviving this encounter unscathed plummeted even further. A growl and a handful of yelping barks emanated from the shadows behind them. Three dog-like shapes slunk into the light. Apparently this Black Annis had control of a pack of Barghests, or demon dogs as they were often called—black, bulky canine monsters with larger than normal teeth that attacked travelers on the road. Their snouts were more blunted than a normal dog but their grip was much tighter when they bit. And they harried their prey endlessly until they killed or were killed themselves.

These beasts were dangerous but mentally weak, sometimes falling under the magical influence of creatures of the night that were more powerful, such as a Black Annis. The supernatural realm was truly growing bold and entering into outright conflict with the Guild if a witch dared to bring her devil pack into the heart of Liverpool.

"Give us the human child, Troll-Man," the witch repeated confidently, "or we will feast on all your flesh instead of just his."

"That will not be possible," Philip responded as calmly as possible. He steadied his nerves and embraced the side of him that relished the fight. He touched it, just beneath the surface, and felt eager anticipation replace the gnawing terror that had threatened when he'd realized the type of witch he was facing.

Philip prepared to fight. Knocking a witch unconscious was always the most crucial thing to accomplish since it nullified all their fighting ability, but when that couldn't be accomplished a more brutal tactic could be employed. Smash the mouth. Without the ability to talk it couldn't cast its spells. However, Black Annises were notoriously hard to put down since they even fought better with their hands than many creatures without magic did. They were doubly dangerous.

The pack of three Barghests advanced on Alayna and Stephen who were behind Philip. As the Barghests made their approach, the witch took a step forward, as well.

"Last chance, Hybrid." The witch's warning was whispered out into the night through chipped teeth. "This is war. The boy is easy pickings and will have information about the Guild here in the city. Information I want. Besides, I'm hungry. But you and the Elfas do not need to die." It dragged out the word die as if savoring it, as if it took dark pleasure in just speaking of death.

"You may find me tougher meat than you think!" Stephen shouted in terrified yet proud anger.

"The lad's right, Witch. We may not go down as easily as you think," Philip said. Just as he said it, Stephen yanked his belt knife out to arm himself and Alayna reached under her cloak to draw out her hidden miniature crossbow. It was not of much use from a distance but it was very effective at close range. She could fire and reload in a heartbeat and then fire again. Philip flexed his fists. He would fight with his preferred strategy—barroom brawl tactics.

Seeing them armed and waiting, the witch snarled and threw off its cloak to free its fighting hands. Her dark hair hung stringy, black, and tangled across her shoulders.

Attacking with lightning speed, it feinted one way and then ducked in close to slash at his legs. Philip felt the bite of steel in his thigh and he swung with all his might, crashing a fist into the chest of the witch, sending it tumbling to clatter into the brick wall of the building, the witch's claws clattering against the stone with a spray of sparks.

Snarling, it furiously picked itself up. It was enraged, and in the moment, Philip oddly wondered if he should think of the witch as a 'she' or an 'it'. He had no time to pursue that line of thought as it began shrieking a string of incantations and hexes. The curses appeared to have no effect on Philip, since he noticed no difference to himself from the magic being cast towards him. The Black Annis grew angrier and muttered filthy words while one clawed finger pointed towards Philip.

"Won't work," he taunted calmly, trying to enrage the Black Annis further. "You should have known that though, since you already seem to know about my trollish origins."

It tossed an evil sneer in his direction and stopped its string of verbal attacks to stalk towards him menacingly again. He stepped forward to meet it, blood flowing from his injured thigh, hoping the wound wouldn't slow him down too greatly. Philip couldn't even spare a glance over his shoulder to see how his companions fared. Splitting his focus against such a dangerous creature would end with him dead in the gutter and likely a meal for the Barghest. He doubted the Black Annis would eat him if he died. The clawed witches preferred their meat younger, the way some men preferred veal to steak.

However, Philip did hear the twang of an arrow being released and the snarling grunt as it struck its target. He prayed that Alayna and Stephen could fend for themselves against the canine attack. His focus had to be the deadly witch in front of him.

He pulled his knife with one hand. He needed something to block the blade-sharp talons of the Black Annis. It advanced on him, eyeing him the way a ridge cat looks at a rabbit. Clearly, it thought it had the advantage. Maybe it did. In fact, Philip was almost certain it did. It was fast and quick, and it wielded the equivalent of ten knives when one considered its ten clawed fingers. Not to mention he was already injured. He would heal after the fight—assuming he survived—faster than any human would, but the wound would certainly slow him down during the actual confrontation.

They met in a clash of edges as his blade parried one hand while the other clawed fingers of the witch tore at his shoulder. The witch was lightning fast! Philip was bleeding even more now and could feel himself slowing by just a step. Philip had to think of a way to end this quickly. He was outmatched and both he and his foe knew it.

An idea began to form.

It was a risky maneuver, to be sure, but it might be his only option. If he did what he was thinking, he would put his healing abilities to the test afterwards in a manner he had never done before. Philip wasn't certain the healing powers he'd inherited from the troll blood in his system would be enough. But either way he had to try. He would likely die if he didn't and this seemed his only real option to defeat the Black Annis and prevent Stephen and Alayna from winding up in its clutches.

He heard a growl and another shriek of inhuman pain as a second arrow found its mark. Time was running out. Alayna wouldn't be able to keep the Barghests at bay for much longer. Maybe if he could kill the witch, the mental control it possessed over the canine monsters would result in their death, as well.

Mind made up, Philip charged and tackled the Black Annis with all his might. He saw the look of surprise as he lunged at the witch in what it clearly assumed to be a suicidal tactic. Philip wasn't sure it was wrong, as the evil glint in the witch's eyes became dark delight as it saw what it believed to be Philip's impending demise. It stretched its hands in front of it, and as the clawed hands met his chest, Philip felt the agonizing bite of ten talons burying themselves deeply into his flesh.

His momentum carried him into the witch with force, which sent them tumbling to the cobblestones in a pile of blood and limbs. After the motion of his tackle and their subsequent roll ended, Philip found himself on top of the witch, face to face with its gleeful expression as it watched him die.

CHAPTER EIGHT

Philip felt the strength draining from his limbs as he lay on top of the Black Annis, his weight pinning it to the ground. It was in no rush to move as it had a face-to-face opportunity to watch him bleed to death. Philip needed to remove those claws from his body and staunch his bleeding if he was to have any chance of surviving. His magical healing abilities just might pull him through, but not if he lay here, bleeding out.

He struggled and the witch just tightened its claws. Philip screamed and his body jerked convulsively. He had made a mistake—this wasn't working! His gamble was going to get him killed. He had to do something, change his predicament somehow.

Philip reached his hands forward, towards the Black Annis' neck, digging deep within himself for whatever strength he still possessed. The witch must have caught a glimpse of determination in his eyes and didn't like it, because suddenly it was the one in a hurry to move. It thrashed, trying to free its hands as Philip's fists closed tightly around its throat. He squeezed to cut off its air supply.

His plan had been to tackle the creature and then trust his added strength of blood to keep him strong enough to break its neck. He had overestimated his own strength. He wasn't powerful enough in his weakened, bleeding state to crush the bones in its neck, but he had just enough energy and life left in his limbs to choke it to death.

The witch wriggled beneath him as it tried to free itself, but its claws were caught fast in the flesh of its attacker. Philip tightened his hands again and the bluish face began to turn purple with lack of air. He smelled the rancid odor of its unwashed body and clothes, the putrid scent of the witch's skin. The Black Annis tried a levitation spell in a last attempt to free itself, but it only managed to lift them an inch or so off the street without being able to breathe and speak the incantation.

Finally, Philip felt the life leave the witch and watched the panic in its eyes glaze over in death. He let go of its neck cautiously and then lifted its head and bashed it to the cobblestones, for good measure.

Philip tried to roll himself off the dead witch but found his muscles were too weak. He moaned and found it hard to talk with the equivalent of ten knives piercing him. His vision was growing fuzzy. The one thing he was aware of was that the sound of barking had ceased. It had worked, the remaining Barghests had died with their mistress.

Two pairs of hands lifted him free of the clawed hands of the Black Annis and then wrapped his navy sea coat tightly around him to try and staunch the bleeding.

The last thing Philip heard before he passed out was the sound of Alayna murmuring worriedly over him.

"Love, what did you do! Why did you do that?"

"I..." Philip couldn't even begin his explanation because the world evaporated around him into nothingness.

———

THE WOUNDS DIDN'T heal overnight. Philip spent three days on his back at Stephen's home. It was the longest he had ever needed to recover from injuries, but then, it was also the gravest he'd ever been wounded in all his time as a Collector. Philip's enhanced healing ability, resulting from the troll blood in his veins, was not a supernatural characteristic that he could control. He couldn't will himself better. In fact, he functioned much like any other unwell person, requiring time and rest for his body to heal itself. In his case, that just happened sooner than it would have for a normal man. It also helped him survive what should have been a life ending confrontation with the Black Annis.

Philip groaned as he sat up from the makeshift invalid bed they had erected in one room of Stephen's home. The pain from his wounds was still there, lurking behind his determination to get moving and proceed with their quest to rescue Beathan. He supposed the pain would remain for some days more even if immediate danger to his life were no longer a concern. Being impaled on ten blade-like claws would do that to a person.

He looked down at his thin, bare chest and saw that while the wounds had mostly healed, they had begun to scar. He'd never scarred this badly before. Perhaps it was due to the gravity of the wounds he endured or maybe there was some sort of magical property to the witch's claws that his troll blood couldn't fully reject, allowing the injuries to leave some sort of mark on him even if they didn't achieve their end goal of his death.

"Easy, Philip," Alayna cautioned, putting a steadying and restraining hand on his shoulder.

Philip struggled to pull on his breeches and then boots, breathing more heavily than he usually would have from such a minor exertion. He sat bare-chested and gazing at Alayna, feeling grateful for the chill breeze swirling into the room through a cracked window. The room was old, the paint on the walls chipping. His companion stood out against the background with her red-gold hair like a rose in a wall of thorns. Philip slowly pulled on his sleeveless tunic over his head and winced as the movement tugged on his freshly healed scars.

"I've never seen you injured like this before. Two days you were in and out of consciousness until you finally turned the corner on the third day. I thought I was going to lose you." Alayna placed a tender hand on his cheek as she stared somberly into his eyes.

"I was never in real danger. It takes more than a tangle with a witch to put me down, love," Philip tried to reassure her with a cheery laugh, but his statement ended in a tiny moan as he felt his chest catch in pain.

Alayna emitted a small, wry chuckle, the one that meant she knew he was lying for her sake. Her mouth twisted up at the corner in a half smile.

"Be that as it may, please don't ever do that to me again." Her words were serious and Philip could feel the love in them.

On his feet at last, he managed to nod and pulled her close into as tight of an embrace as he could manage without causing too much pain. He would have to move slowly and take things very easy for the next few days until his body fully completed the healing process.

But he reminded himself to be thankful. Most people, even those with supernatural abilities, would have been dead after what he went through fighting the Black Annis, but all Philip could feel was impatience. Three days wasted on his back, and all the while Beathan rotted in a cell. It galled him to imagine it.

The two of them walked out of the room and into the common quarters of Stephen's home where the lad was arranging an array of tools and weapons. To a normal person, it would have been a veritable arsenal, but to Philip it was the bare minimum a Collector could hope to have at his disposal. Still, it was a sight for sore eyes after six months with little other than his fists and a small belt knife to protect himself.

Stephen looked up from what he was doing. "Sir, I know you didn't ask, but I couldn't help but think you might be needing some of these." His hand swept in a gesture to the weapons laid out on the floor. "It's not much, but it's what I could get from the Guild outpost without them being suspicious."

Philip took a closer look and saw that most of the weapons were worn with use. Still good enough to be dangerous, but not the sort of weapons the Guild would send out with a formally employed Collector. A few blades had rust, and some dust was collecting on the outsides of a few small bottles of liquid—no doubt some sort of herbalized potion. It was more than he'd had a moment ago so it would have to do.

"It's wonderful, Stephen," he said thanking the boy with a hand on his shoulder. Stephen grinned up at Philip, glad to be of service.

"You do too much," Alayna said with a fond smile for the boy.

Philip agreed with her. "Yes, lad, promise me you'll pinch nothing else from the Guild's storeroom, even if it is old, unused gear. I don't want you in trouble on our account."

"Nothing else," Stephen promised solemnly, although there was a twinkle of mischief in his eye that reminded Philip of his old partner. James had been a Guild man to his core, but he had flouted the rules on more occasions than one. Whenever it suited his purposes, actually. Philip wondered if that was the type of Collector Stephen would become.

They spent one more day in Stephen's company before arranging passage on a ship south. Philip found a discreet sea captain leaving Liverpool that day, one with a penchant for making money on the side in a less than legal way. When Philip told the man that they had a lucrative proposition for him that would require only a drop off and a pick up at two separate locations, the man had jumped at the offer.

While packing up their meager gear at Stephen's home, Philip and Alayna made their goodbyes. Philip put a worn silver knife into the satchel full of weapons, then a vial of river water—good for deterring vampires. There were a few stakes and some herbs, as well, to stuff into the bag. All in all it wasn't much, but beggars couldn't be choosers.

The lad walked them to the harbor until they reached their vessel for passage. Stephen felt sad, Philip could tell. Even with the danger, the boy must have enjoyed a familiar face. He wondered what type of men the lad was working for that caused him to feel so lonely. Thirteen was a young age to be caught up in this mess.

The life of an apprentice wasn't that of a normal youth. Work instead of play, and often for men who were much more focused on the job than on caring for the emotional needs of their apprentice. Philip himself had been much the same way when Stephen first came to work for him and James. But there was nothing Philip could do now. He had a task ahead of him, a monumental breakout to accomplish. He couldn't do anything for Stephen now. Besides, despite his loyalty to Philip—and Philip could see that there was a genuine trust and companionship between himself and Stephen—the boy was still Guild. The lad was Guild down to his bootstraps.

They were on different sides of a steadily increasing conflict. Who knew what might happen if they crossed paths years down the road. Philip pushed that thought from his mind. He might not even survive the month if his plans went awry in rescuing the fairy. Focus on today he thought to himself, and leave tomorrow for tomorrow.

Stephen broke his contemplation. "You should've died, Master Philip," the boy said keenly. "Those wounds were the nastiest I've ever seen. Yet here you stand, hardly the worse for wear."

Philip appraised him silently. The boy was entirely too clever at times.

"Don't worry, Sir. I won't tell them." They both knew that the *them* he was referring to was the Collectors Guild. Perhaps the boy wasn't Guild down to his core as Philip had thought.

He smiled and ruffled Stephen's shaggy hair in unspoken thanks, while staying silent and not admitting to anything. But the look they shared was a knowing one. Alayna had spoken truth on the ship. You could only hide who you were for so long before eventually your true identity revealed itself.

Philip changed the subject, not wanting to discuss delicate issues with the boy. The less Stephen actually knew about Philip the safer he was in the long run. "Lad, you may want to consider staying in the Guild compound from now on. That Black Annis may not be the last supernatural being with the idea that an apprentice might be an easy capture in order to gain information on the Guild outpost here in the city. If things really are heating up into a full-scale conflict, some precautions will be necessary."

"I will, Sir," the boy promised somberly. "I'd be dead if you hadn't been there the other night. I don't plan on that happening again." He sounded old for his age now, not the chattering boy who had been so eager to see his old master and friend returned from the dead.

Well, Philip shouldn't be surprised. The Guild had a way of aging a youth faster than average. War had a way of doing that to people. Even at the best of times, when conflict between the Guild and the supernatural realm was not at an outright rampage, it was still dangerous. It was always a war, Philip realized, sometimes it came to a boil, and other times it was only at a low simmer. It didn't have to be that way, but it was. And it likely always would be.

With the last important words spoken, Philip clasped the lad in a rough embrace, his eyes watering up unexpectedly. Who knew when or if he would see the lad again? Alayna grasped the boy's hand in an affectionate goodbye and then they boarded the ship headed for the south of England.

CHAPTER NINE

The cell was dark and dank. It smelled of rats and feces. In general, it was everything Beathan expected a cell would be. And he hated it with every fiber of his being.

He barely remembered arriving at St. Thomas's. The Collectors must have decided he was more dangerous than previously thought after his escape attempt, and had begun drugging him. It had turned the rest of his journey by ship into a fog of delirium, days and nights that blended into one another without any real definition where one ended and the other began. But he was here now, in St. Thomas's, of that much he was sure. His head was clearing and it wouldn't be long before they came in to drug him again. They must have realized he had magical ability not just supernatural physical attributes and were determined to make sure their captive couldn't activate his charms. It was too difficult to use his charms and spells when he couldn't think straight enough to speak. Words to activate his magic seemed like they would be too much effort right now.

His head lolled over, as his neck was too weak from the drugs to keep it upright. He looked down at his wrists and saw they were chained to the floor rather than above his head like they had been in the wagon. At least there was that small convenience. He could at least accept his current state of imprisonment in a more comfortable position than the journey here.

Beathan's eyes stayed glued to his wrists and he saw the shallow cuts.

Memory served him and he remembered. They were bleeding him. It wasn't enough just to drug him and dull his senses, they were bleeding him in carefully measured amounts to ensure he remained in a weakened state. A headache throbbed in his temple. He wasn't sure if it was a result of drugs or the blood loss. He wished it would go away, but the aching pain remained.

He found it hard to move his head again, so weak was his neck, but finally he managed to loll it back in the other direction to survey the other side of his cell. It was dark and windowless, somewhere deep in the bedrock below the Guild prison masquerading as a monastery. A faint light crept in through the rusty, barred gate that served as an entrance and barrier. There must be a torch somewhere in the distant recesses of this gloomy, underground hell, Beathan thought.

A noise caught his attention, a rustling of clothes as limbs moved. He peered across the way from him, and as his eyes grew keener as they adjusted to the dimness, he saw it was Azir. They had been separated on the ship, kept in different parts of the hold. Beathan had assumed it would be the same here at St. Thomas's. Apparently not. It appeared he had company.

"Can a person not get their own cell around here?" he asked in mock indignation. "Ya'd think they were fixin' to make us the best o' friends." The joke rebounded weakly off the rough-hewn stone walls of the cell.

"You do not want to be my friend, Fairy. It would be better for you if you were not." Azir muttered his response and Beathan saw that he seemed to be in no better condition than Beathan. He leaned weakly against the wall a few yards away across the cell. Although, on second thought, his weakness appeared to be from something other than drugs since Beathan could tell there was a keenness in the Elfas' eyes that drugs would have dulled had they been administered to Azir.

"Doesn't look like I have many options, now do I?" Beathan quipped back, toying with his new ring, the charmed one he'd discovered and stolen at the market just before capture. The manacles provided enough leeway to bring his hands together in order to do so. A steady drip, drip, drip trickled down from the ceiling and landed on the back of Beathan's hand. He tried reaching out to discern what magic the charmed ring possessed but his mind was too foggy to accomplish much.

He stared across his cell and looked at Azir. The pale tone of the Elfas skin looked almost ashy now but Beathan figured it must be the lighting. However, the Elfas' face looked even thinner and more hollowed than the last time Beathan had really looked at it in the wagon before his escape attempt. The Elfas' dark eyes glinted in the gloom.

"I do love the dark, but oh, how I hate these chains," Azir whispered as if talking to himself. Hopefully capture hadn't driven him mad.

Beathan frowned. "I didn't know your kind had such an affinity for darkness. Moonlight, starlight surely, but not the utter blackness one experiences below ground."

Azir smiled grimly and for some reason it gave Beathan a chill. "There is much you do not know about me and my... kind." Azir responded in his typical, secretive fashion.

Beathan kept fiddling with his new charm ring idly. He managed to remember an all-purpose spell that might be able to induce the charm's ability, at least to a minor extent. He muttered the incantation while touching the ring and channeling his magic through it and then waited. A drop of water fell from the ceiling and then rebounded off an unseen obstacle above his hand. He stopped the spell and the trickle resumed its natural course of falling upon his exposed skin.

Interesting.

Some kind of defensive charm to block attacks perhaps? However, Beathan had no more time to ponder and explore the charm's ability because a guard's footsteps padded in the direction of their cell. The rusted, barred gate squeaked open and a burly Collector quickly overwhelmed Beathan's weak struggles and pressed a funnel into the fairy's mouth. Beathan felt the cool, bitter liquid pour into his mouth and down his throat as he was forced to swallow. The fog in his brain increased immediately as the drugs took instant effect. The guard turned to leave without trying to drug Azir. Apparently the Elfas didn't have enough magic to warrant such special treatment.

In a flash of movement, Azir had stood up and burst to the furthest reach that his chains allowed, thrashing and snapping his jaws like a madman at the guard. However, the chains held and restrained him. Beathan could swear, even through his growing grogginess, that the Elfas' teeth were longer.

The guard just chuckled. "No, no, pet. I'll have none of your tantrums. My blood is not for you." And then he swung the iron door shut with a clang and clumped back in the other direction. Azir collapsed in the grime of the cell floor, a puddle of exhaustion, as if the Elfas had used every ounce of his remaining strength in the burst of energy it had taken to try and attack the guard.

Azir shook his head dizzily almost in confusion. "I shouldn't have tried that. Wasteful of my energy," he mumbled. "But I'm so thirsty, so parched!" His throaty whisper pierced the stillness of the cell just as realization dawned on Beathan's drugged mind.

"Have ya' completed the transition yet, Azir?" Beathan asked dreading the answer he knew he would receive.

———

"WHAT DO YOU MEAN?" Azir asked, and then said, "I am not sure I follow." His eastern accent seemed a cliché now that Beathan realized what was happening.

"Ya' know what I mean," Beathan responded firmly, "Are ya'still in the process or have ya' finished transitionin' into a vampire?"

Azir stared at Beathan for a moment then decided to give up the charade. For a split second Beathan thought he saw a flash of shame on the vampire's face but then instead Azir answered with a sneer on his face. "It is done. My body has accepted the transition. If only I could drink now! My untimely capture was most unfortunate. These last days have been torture. Especially now, when the blood pumping in your veins and leaking out your wrists is so tantalizingly close." He stared hungrily at Beathan and licked his lips with a delicate tongue.

Beathan shook his head in disbelief. Why had Azir chosen this fate? A person had to choose to accept the bite of a vampire in order for it to turn you. They weren't contagious the way werewolves were. For someone to become a vampire they had to determine in their heart, in their consciousness, that they desired such a life. A life of blood and the lust to drink.

Pity clouded his thoughts. He couldn't help but feel bad for the Elfas. He supposed he should think of him as a vampire now. Or was he a hybrid? Many vampires relished in the kill, in the dark beauty of a sweetly taken life. Yet, there were some who found their new existence not altogether what they had expected. It remained to be seen which type of vampire Azir would become. Although, it was clear from the way he spoke and the manner in which he was eyeing Beathan's injured wrists where the Collectors had bled him, that he was indeed experiencing the bloodlust.

"Do not look at me in that way!" Azir practically snarled at Beathan from across the stone cage deep in the bowels of England.

"In what way?"

"With pity." The newly formed vampire practically spit his words now. "I chose this. I wanted this life. Do not pity me!"

"I know ya' did. It couldn't have happened any other way. But just because ya' decided freely on an ill fate does not mean that I cannot pity you. Some o' the worst decisions are a direct result of free will." Beathan tilted his head and looked regretfully at the vampire.

"I chose this. I wanted it..." the vampire trailed off as if realizing he was only repeating himself.

"When?" Beathan asked, curiosity getting the better of him.

Azir looked away as if wishing to tell his story without having to watch Beathan's face as he did so. Maybe he was already regretting his choice. His emotions on the subject seemed conflicted, one moment glad of his decision and the next regretful.

"A little over a week gone now. I had a vampire who owed me—I'd done her a favor once and we were on... friendlier terms than most people are with vampires." Azir smirked slightly as he spoke. Clearly the relationship had been of a romantic nature. At least, to whatever degree a vampire could be romantically inclined. Beathan wasn't exactly sure about the issue, but he did know the bloodlust they experienced could be all consuming. It couldn't be easy to find romance in the midst of another overwhelming passion. More likely their relationship had been sexual in nature.

"Anyway, she accepted my request for the bite. She left soon after, her debt repaid, and well for her that she did because no sooner had she gone then the place was swarming with Collectors." Azir paused for a moment as if wondering how to proceed with his story. He shifted the chains on his wrists slightly as if to ease the chafing. Beathan waited silently for him to continue. He found a dark fascination with the former Elfas' tale.

The vampire continued. "The bite does not change you immediately. It takes you in an out of consciousness, like dreaming and then waking and then dreaming again. I was hardly in a lucid state when the Collectors arrived and bagged me." Azir pursed his lips sourly, bitterly. "I did not even put up a fight. The next thing I knew I was in the wagon, and there you were slumped across from me."

That semi-dreaming state explained why he'd not been able to wake Azir before the ill-fated escape attempt. A pity the vampire hadn't been conscious. Perhaps the two of them might have been able to escape if the transition hadn't gotten in the way of Azir joining the fray. Then again, maybe it was for the best. The way Azir was staring intently at Beathan's neck, made the fairy wonder if perhaps the vampire would have just as likely attacked him out of desire for his first feed as fought beside him against the Collectors. Who knew how sane a new vampire was, especially when it hadn't had a chance to feed yet. It might leap at the first handy opportunity to bite a victim, regardless of the timing or circumstances.

Beathan decided a little more prying wouldn't hurt. "So tell me, mate, how did ya' manage to be contactin' me friend, Alayna, when I asked? I didn't know the vampiric nature allowed for mind t' mind conversation."

"I was still in the process of transitioning. Some of my mental faculties had not deserted me yet. Although," the vampire narrowed his eyes in contemplation, "I can still feel some of my old nature as an Elfas mixed in with the new desires that burn within me." Azir seemed pleased at this mix.

"Can I ask why ya' did it?" Beathan's curiosity still had not been assuaged.

"Why?" Azir asked with an incredulous laugh as if he could not believe Beathan needed to ask. "I am a hybrid now, fairy. I am special, different. I am more than I was before. More powerful. Most vampires are simply that—vampires. They lose their old nature. But that is because most were humans and the human mind is weak."

His disgust for human strength of will was clear from the sneer on his face. "It is easily consumed by the new nature. I am—was—an Elfas, and my mind was peerless even then. There was no guarantee that I would become what I am now—a hybrid, but I knew the likelihood of my old nature to survive, to join with my new nature, was much greater than for other people. It was a risk. I had never heard of a vampire turned from an Elfas, and death was a possibility—that my body might reject the change. But I had faith that I could survive and become something greater."

Beathan could practically hear the arrogance dripping in Azir's voice. He certainly thought a lot of himself. However, Beathan had to admit it did take courage to commit to the unknown. Azir had essentially experimented on himself. And he had done it fearlessly.

Nevertheless, Beathan couldn't help but take a jab at the vampire Elfas. Sometimes it was good to deflate an ego. "Well, lot o' good it did ya', your fancy experimentin'. Got ya' locked up in a cell with me." He grinned.

Surprisingly, Azir laughed. He was egotistical and proud, but apparently he had a sense of humor and appreciated the comedy of an ironic situation.

"Yes Fairy, here I am. With you in this godforsaken pit of a cell. But, I have a feeling I will not be here forever. After all, you had me contact your friend for a reason, did you not?"

"True, Azir, I did have ya' send the mental message. But it remains t' be seen if that attempt will pay off."

"Oh, I made contact with her, Beathan. She knows where we are, I could sense it. And what a precious mind it was—I could tell that even in the midst of my transition, even though our mental connection was tainted by the insurgence of my vampire nature. I do hope it did not leave too nasty a mark on her consciousness." Azir had a sly look on his face and Beathan felt a chill wondering what he had subjected Alayna to by forcing Azir on her. The vampire was unpredictable at best. One moment he seemed friendly, the next dangerous and hinting at dark pleasures and evil desires. Beathan hoped he had not made too grave a mistake by involving him. But what choice had he had?

"I must admit it feels good to be a hybrid. I can feel both of my natures coinciding into greater power, the way two waves meet in the ocean and often form a larger wave as a result." Azir seemed pleased with himself at the moment. Any trace of shame from earlier was gone. Perhaps it had been Beathan's imagination.

"Ya' know, I'm a half-breed also," Beathan volunteered, his head feeling fuzzy again as the story ended and his brain lost focus due to the drugs in his system.

"A cross between what?" The vampire seemed genuinely interested.

"Fairy, human, and some leprechaun way back on me ma's side o' the family."

The vampire assumed a dismissive expression. "Humans are weak. Your blood is little more than what I would call polluted."

"Never looked at it in such a way," Beathan disagreed but without much conviction. He was finding it harder to think straight as the drugs began to take true hold over his system.

Suddenly, Azir laughed a real laugh without any of his darker attributes creeping in to influence his humor. "Leprechaun, you say? Not to be crude, but how on earth did that work? Is it even possible for them to mate with another species?"

Beathan gave him a cheerful look. "Well now, that's quite a story to tell. Suffice to say, mate, that it involves a wee bit of a lass and a giant of a leprechaun. He came up past her hips in height. 'Twas massive for a green man. Was a match made in heaven!" He winked at Azir and he could tell the vampire didn't know if he was serious or joking. He liked it that way. It was always best to keep people on their toes around you, never certain of what you meant. A little mystery went a long way in maintaining a reputation.

"You cannot be serious," Azir said incredulously.

"Can't I?" Beathan asked with a half-cocked, drug-addled grin.

CHAPTER TEN

"We will enter through a sewage pipe that runs down through the inside of the cliff and meets the water." Philip was describing to Alayna the plan he had concocted.

"It doesn't sound too difficult, Philip. It's surprising that nobody has tried it before." Alayna's response was more or less what he'd expected.

"Well, that's sort of true, Alayna. However, the pipe at the bottom is barred with an iron grate. The bars are fit together too narrowly for anyone to enter. I'll have to hope that I'm strong enough to force them apart in order to give us entrance."

They were a few hours from destination, off the southern coast of England. The trip south from Liverpool had been largely uneventful. It had consisted mainly of Philip—under Alayna's orders—resting and recovering. Basically it meant lolling about on the bunk and occasionally stretching his legs with a quick jaunt up on deck.

Now he sat with Alayna in the cabin they'd purchased for the trip. "However, getting in to St. Thomas's may not be entirely easy—our entry point requires someone of supernatural strength—but on the whole, the difficulty of breaking into the prison has never been its main deterrent. Now, escaping on the other hand..." He trailed off.

Alayna nodded her understanding and said, "I see. It's like a trap? Getting in isn't the hard part but once you're in, it's difficult to escape it. So, what's our exit strategy?"

"Exiting will not be our main problem either. Or at least it shouldn't be," Philip answered. "We'll go out the way we came in—the sewage pipe."

"So, what's the issue?" Alayna turned quizzical eyes to Philip.

Philip grimaced. "The difficulty is getting out unnoticed. In fact, it's impossible."

"Impossible?" Alayna raised her eyebrows in surprise.

"Impossible." Philip confirmed seriously. "No matter what happens, the Guild workers and guards at St. Thomas's will know we are there and will be hot in pursuit even if we make a clean getaway."

"I'm sensing there is something about the jail you haven't told me before now." Alayna had a keen insight into issues left unspoken. She'd always had the talent to see to the heart of matters.

Philip held her gaze as he spoke, wanting to impress the seriousness of the situation. "The Guild is not above hypocrisy. We—they," Philip amended the unconscious slip of the tongue, "They hunt and capture or kill the supernatural, those they deem dangerous to humankind. However, they are not above using magic themselves in the process. Of course, the average Collector will not use anything beyond simple, if crafty, tools and weapons. Yet, the heart of what the Guild represents is embodied in St. Thomas's. The prison stands for separation and even punishment of the creatures that pose a threat to people all over the world.

"It is not always just—certainly Beathan does not deserve to be held in its stony walls. But to the Guild, if there were ever a failure to hold what had been transported there, some of the most dangerous individuals and creatures the world has ever known would be set loose. They cannot allow that to happen."

Alayna was listening intently. "So they bend their own rules in this one place. They use magic to ensure that magic is locked away." For a moment Philip was distracted by her full lips as she spoke. She could always manage to distract him, even in serious situations. And she likely didn't even realize she was doing it. He laughed silently in his head, but tried to focus and finish his explanation.

Alayna was asking another question. "So what kind of magic do they use to protect St. Thomas's, Philip?"

"There are a variety of obstacles of which to be wary, but the most relevant to us are the sensor spells that cover every inch of the grounds. Every guard and prisoner is spelled so that the sensor spells will recognize them and not set the alarm. However, an intruder will trip those magical alarms the instant they set foot inside the prison." As Philip spoke, he heard the insanity of what they were about to attempt. Every guard in the building would be converging upon them in minutes as soon as they entered through the pipe.

"Who is responsible for casting such spells?" Alayna's inquisitiveness kept Philip talking.

There was a lot to tell a layperson about St. Thomas's. Philip had been in to the prison to drop prisoners off, but he'd only been temporarily spelled when he'd entered. Only the guards were spelled permanently along with those they guarded. It was the Guild's precautionary tactics to ensure the prison stayed as impregnable as possible.

Philip kept answering her questions as she asked. "There are mages loyal to the Guild, men and women, not unlike Astori, who through one means or another came to possess magical abilities. Only, they maintained their fidelity to the organization because they believe in its cause, unlike Astori, who revolted. These mages are the ones who spell the prison." He paused as he thought of how to say the next part.

"What is it, love? I can see there's more you want to tell me." Alayna grasped his hand to let him know she was fine, not overwhelmed by the danger and immensity of the task ahead.

"Mages and warding spells aren't the only hypocrisy the Guild perpetuates."

Alayna tilted her head in question at Philip's statement.

Philip continued. "The Guild also keeps... domesticated monsters as guards, creatures that are loosed should there ever be an escape or rescue attempt. They are called Deadbloods and are bound through magic to serve the Guild and its ends."

"I see. So they really have covered all their angles. Magic to counteract magic, beasts to counter the supernatural beings who might attempt an escape." Alayna murmured as if she were still thinking her way through it all.

Philip nodded. "You can see why St. Thomas's has developed such an unsavory, even hopeless, reputation in the supernatural world. Nobody even attempts what we are about to do because most people are realistic enough to recognize that it is likely a suicide mission."

"So what makes it different for us?" Alayna's latest question was a pertinent one.

Philip had to be honest with her. "Not a lot, love. I know about the drainage pipe, which is hidden, and has an exit point that is at the base of the cliff and often covered with water. So, that gives us one advantage of which most wouldn't be aware. I've also been inside so I'm somewhat familiar with the layout of the prison. But to be completely frank, Alayna, there's a reason nobody we know of has broken out of St. Thomas's—because it's incredibly hard to do. It will not be any different for us."

They sat in silence for a few minutes as Philip let the information sink in. Finally, he had to speak. "You don't have to do this, Alayna. In fact, I'd prefer you didn't. You don't have to risk yourself for a suicide mission."

Iron resolve formed on her face and Philip's heart dropped. For a moment he had thought he might be able to convince her not to join him on this foolhardy mission.

"We Alderfolk may not be great fighters or the most dangerous, but we pay our debts. I owe Beathan my life, just as you do, and I plan to see him safely out of there. Besides, you'll need someone to watch your back. You are hardly invincible, Philip, as we have clearly seen from our last skirmish in Liverpool. You need me." Alayna was determined to come along—it was clear from her words. Philip nodded his acceptance silently.

Philip was conflicted internally. He knew she was right, an extra set of fighting hands would likely be necessary inside the prison, but he was loathe to put her in that kind of danger. However, it wasn't his choice. She wanted to come along. He had never told her what to do and he wouldn't start now. If they were to perish in this dangerous escape attempt, at least they would be together.

———

THE SHIP WAS ROUNDING the point, about to sail past the cove where St. Thomas's was located. But the ship wouldn't stop and drop anchor there. Philip didn't want anything unusual to alert the Guild that they were coming. Instead, he and Alayna would jump overboard as the ship kept sailing and would swim to the base of the cliff where the drainage pipe was located. The ship would wait for them down the coast a short ways, out of sight of the Guild and the prison.

The captain, a man who called himself by the name of Dimsby—although Philip was almost certain that wasn't his real name, based on his shifty eyes and suspicious demeanor—had agreed to drop anchor and wait. He clearly had done his fair share of less than legitimate business in his day and as a former or perhaps current smuggler, he wasn't one to pass up an easy profit.

Philip and Alayna would swim ashore and then meet up with him later to pay him the second half of what he was owed. He would wait a day and if they didn't return, then he was free to go, having made an easy profit. It was a risk. He might decide to leave them and be happy with what he had already been paid, but he had a greedy look and Philip was fairly sure he'd want the second half of the payment.

As the cliffs on which St. Thomas's was built appeared, Philip's gaze trailed upwards to the average looking church building on top. It was emblematic of the Guild, really. The Guild was always average looking with much more to show beneath the surface.

Philip, himself, was a perfect example. As a Collector, he had looked extremely ordinary but had been trained for years in preparation for a dangerous profession. Strangers would not have looked twice at him or thought him anything other than an average working man. St. Thomas's prison was the same. To the unsuspecting eye it was a simple monastery above ground, but below, it was a cavernous expanse of tunnels and levels with cells beyond count.

Readying themselves to jump, Philip turned to Alayna with a questioning glance. She'd been quiet during the past few hours since he'd explained to her just how difficult and dangerous their task really was.

"Last chance to reconsider." He hoped she would, but knew she wouldn't.

"Of course not," she replied dismissively, in as confident a voice as she could muster. Yet, Philip could see the nerves just below the surface of her calm exterior. At times it was difficult to remember that not everyone had lived their life working a job that required them to risk their life on a weekly if not daily basis.

Until a half year ago, Alayna had lived a simple life in the countryside. He felt nerves, of course. He always had, but he had also always been able to mask those fears and control them, channel them into caution and guile that helped him survive in a dangerous world. He might not feel that same fear now—his wild heritage actually had him looking forward to what he knew was likely to be combat once they entered the prison—but he could remember what it had been like.

Alayna wasn't human any longer, but her new people were not warlike.

He was proud of the courage it must be requiring of her to undertake this rescue attempt with him.

"One last thing," Alayna murmured, grabbing his hand and delaying their departure over the rail of the ship. They would jump off the far side so that a chance eye from the cliff would not see two souls disembarking into the water of the cove. Once they were wet and swimming, roving eyes were not likely to notice them, as the ship sailing onwards would draw attention away from them.

Alayna squeezed his hand tightly.

"What?" Philip asked hoping to dispel any last fears as best as he could before they began.

Alayna smiled ruefully, noticing the vice grip she'd had on his callused hand. "Sorry, a few nerves I guess. I was just wondering, what exactly are the guard monsters—what did you call them? Deadbloods?—that you mentioned before? You sort of glossed over them earlier."

Philip grimaced. This wasn't likely to calm her. In fact, it would probably have the opposite effect. But there was nothing he could do but answer her now and trust she could handle the information.

"They are creatures that have been caught and then killed. The mages of which I spoke earlier are populated by a specific type of magician called a Blood Mage. The Blood Mages cast spells on the blood and enliven the dead beings, giving health and vitality once again to the blood that runs through the creature's veins. It is a difficult magic, and one for which the mages have trained all of their time. They are masters at one or two types of magic and not much else, but that is what the Guild desires of them."

"They resurrect the dead? Are you saying that the Collectors Guild, the secret organization that hunts, kills, and captures all manner of magical and dangerous beings, world wide, has an army of undead at their disposal?" The incredulity in her voice was understandable. It was quite a paradox of values by the Guild.

"Well, not really an army. There are a limited number of Blood Mages and they can only control a few of the Deadbloods each so it's more like a small company of beasts at their command rather than an entire army." He tried to lighten the mood with a joking grin, but he could tell the news had shaken Alayna slightly. Learning that you were about to break into a prison filled with resurrected monsters could do that to you.

"But essentially yes, love, they do control the dead. The Deadbloods are raised back to life with the magic of the Blood Mages flowing in their blood, flowing through them. But they are not really alive, nor are they dead. They are something in between. They must return at the end of each day to the Blood Mage who controls them in order to have the spell cast all over again.

"Without it, their blood ceases to give life and they revert to their previously deceased state of being. They are sentient and more or less have control of their minds in much the same manner as when they were alive—if perhaps just slightly more malleable mentally—yet they are slaves to the magic of the mages. They must do what they are commanded, to guard and protect the prison, or they will be forced to die again."

Alayna shuddered. "I almost wish I hadn't asked. The undead are not something one can accept lightly."

Philip nodded understandingly. It was a lot to come to terms with, he knew. He'd had a lifetime to learn about all the nuances of the Guild. It was all new to Alayna. They had not often talked about the Guild in the half year they'd been traveling and living together in the wild. They had preferred to focus on more immediate and joyful subjects, such as the present and the future, not Philip's past.

It was time.

"Ready?" Philip questioned Alayna as the ship reached the optimal point along the outskirts of the cove for the two of them to disembark.

Alayna shook her head slightly and Philip thought the latest piece of information might have surprised and frightened her enough to reconsider. But then he realized she was instead shaking herself from whatever dark reverie their conversation had induced. She turned her head to face him and spoke with her usual confidence.

"Ready."

They let go of each other's hands and then dove over the rail of the ship together. Philip hit the water in a clean dive, not creating much of a splash and felt the shock of cold slam into his frame. The salty wetness penetrated his whole body. Luckily, he could tolerate the cold. Alayna, on the other hand, must be freezing.

Alayna came up for air after her entry into the water, her strawberry blonde locks clinging to her head. She had a grin of excitement, as if the nerves she'd clearly been experiencing on the ship were now forgotten in the anticipation of a mission to be completed.

They treaded water and waited for the ship to sail by, giving them enough of a clear path to swim to shore. When it was time, Philip started out with smooth, strong strokes. He had always been a competent swimmer. He'd spent enough time over the years with James sailing the Atlantic, that inevitably opportunities to swim presented themselves.

Alayna kept pace, pulling her lithe, body through the ocean with ease. They swam for what felt like forever. The cliffs rose high above the shore, making land appear deceptively closer than it really was. But they swam onward, ignoring the cold as best they could until they reached the base of the cliff beneath St. Thomas's.

Philip ducked under the swells that threatened to push them against the rocky cliff face while Alayna treaded water, waiting. He took a deep breath and plunged himself into the murky water, searching for the pipe that would give them access. Eventually he found it, a few yards beneath the waves. On a very low tide it would likely be clear of the water, which was the time when the Guild would use it to expel refuse. However, the majority of the time this entry point into the prison was hidden beneath the surf and surge of the ocean.

"It's over here," he said quietly to Alayna a few feet away. He motioned her over.

"What now?" Her lips were turning a light shade of blue. Not life threatening, but it would be good to get her out of the water and moving soon. Climbing up the shaft would warm her muscles.

"Now, we see if I'm strong enough to get us inside."

Philip dove under the water again and reached the iron grate blocking the pipe's exit. He put both hands to the sides of two bars and strained outward with his arms using all of his supernatural might. Nothing. Or at least no perceptible movement of the bars. His lungs were burning with the effort of exertion while holding his breath and he surfaced with a gasp. He sucked in air and dove back down.

This time the bars gave just slightly as he pulled them apart. He strained and struggled until dark spots floated across his vision before surfacing again. He coughed up a mouthful of seawater that he had accidentally swallowed while surfacing.

"Any luck?" Alayna asked tensely. She knew as well as he did that the longer they stayed there bobbing around at the base of the cliff, the more likely they were to be spotted.

"One more attempt should be sufficient. I think I can bend the bars just enough to allow one person through at a time."

He submerged himself again and true to his conjecture the bars warped slightly under his powerful hands and arms. It definitely allowed enough room for Alayna to fit through, and Philip was slender and lean for a man, so he hoped it would be wide enough for him to enter.

He poked his head back above the waves. "Alright, we're ready. I'll go first just follow me. And try not to fall, it will slow us down."

They dove down together and Philip approached the grate. He turned his body sideways and entered the pipe at an angle surfacing in the tiny shaft. Alayna's head rose above the water too. They were almost on top of each other in the small space. Anyone who disliked tiny areas would probably panic squeezing into a shaft like this with someone else.

"This is cozy," Alayna nipped playfully at his lip, and Philip couldn't help but laugh. Their bodies were pressed close together in the ocean water and he could feel the curves of her form. Perhaps he wasn't the only one who got distracted.

"Cozy, but it doesn't exactly smell romantic." Philip wrinkled his nose. They were in a refuse pipe after all. Alayna's silvery laugh pealed quietly. But she didn't say anything else.

Time to climb. The pipe was man-made, but it was nothing more than a rough-hewn shaft in the rock. There were handholds aplenty as well as many areas on which to scrape your joints. The walls of the shaft were slick with grime and Philip tried not to think about what coated the walls, what waste was disposed of through this shaft at low tide. He leveraged himself higher and higher. They climbed in silence until they finally reached the top. Philip found himself looking upwards at soft torchlight flickering on stone walls above him. They had reached the inside of St. Thomas!

He turned his head to look at Alayna and whispered, "Here we go." As an afterthought, he whispered, "There's bound to be some fighting before this is over but try not to kill anything that doesn't deserve it." He didn't think the statement was necessary with Alayna, but it didn't hurt to make sure. He was no longer a Collector, not one of the Guild, but he didn't want to see guards dead if it was avoidable.

With that he swung himself up and out of the chute and onto the hard stone floor of the prison. It wasn't more than a few moments until Alayna landed at his side.

They hadn't gone more than a few feet from the hole in the wall before a bell began to toll, clanging loudly and proclaiming the presence of intruders. Philip knew that just as he had expected, their very presence inside the walls of the prison was enough to set off the sensor spells that warded every inch of this place.

Philip felt his pulse quicken and his blood race as he and Alayna moved as silently as possible through the lowest levels of the caverns of St. Thomas. Where was Beathan? They had to find Beathan quickly and escape back to the sewage pipe or this venture would end in utter disaster.

CHAPTER ELEVEN

Philip moved quickly along the narrow corridors of the bottom level of St. Thomas's. The prison was a rabbit warren of tunnels connecting walkways with cave-like cells. The light was faint, only the wavering luminescence of torches lit the way. Rough stonewalls yielded to uneven floors. St. Thomas's had been excavated into the rocky interior of the cliff on which the monastery was erected, but little had been done to smooth the stony footpaths that crisscrossed the expanse of the prison.

Alayna followed quietly, staying close to Philip, and all the while the tolling of the bell sounded, a faint clanging above them. Philip peered into each of the cells they passed. Some were empty, but most were occupied. A muzzled witch hissed and gurgled at him from behind a contraption that prevented her from speaking. It was a classic Guild tactic. If a witch couldn't talk then it couldn't cast spells on you. It was part of the reason why choking the Black Annis in Liverpool had been so effective.

Onwards and deeper into the gloom of the jail they continued. A werewolf in one cell was raving and clawing at the wall of his earthen cage with bloody human fingers. It wasn't a full moon so the werewolf was relatively harmless in human form. It was clearly mad—a common side effect of the werewolf virus—and had long since ceased its connection with reality. In one cell Philip saw what looked like a man, and for a moment, he almost spoke and called out Beathan's name. But then the skin of the creature shifted slightly, like an illusion wavering in the light of day, and a faun's form filled Philip's sight.

"Help me," it cajoled, rattling its manacles as it tried to stagger towards him. As it moved closer he saw it was bloody and beaten, with lacerations along its arms and bare chest.

Philip furrowed his brow. Those injuries didn't look self-inflicted. He didn't remember the guards at St. Thomas being allowed to torture their captives. Apparently circumstances had changed. His thoughts were confirmed by the sight of a vampire sitting on the floor of its cell, staring through the rusted iron bars with glazed eyes. Both its legs were broken and contorted at painfully odd angles.

St. Thomas had indeed grown darker in Philip's absence. He had never spent much time within its walls, but a biannual trip to unload a haul of captives had allowed him to see it, however infrequently. It had never been like this.

A lot had transpired in the past year since he had been here. To him and to the prison. It resembled more of a house of torture than a secure prison now. A wail of agony joined the tolling of the alarm bell as if to punctuate his thought. It made his lip curl just looking at what had been done to some of the residents. Suddenly, it occurred to Philip that it didn't matter that many of them were likely evil and dangerous. This was horrible. It was a disgusting way to treat living beings. But there was no time to do anything about it. He had to find Beathan and escape as quickly as possible, otherwise the same fate awaited him and Alayna.

He picked up his pace, eager to leave this hell as soon as he could. The stench of rotted food and refuse filled his nose as they hurried past a barrel filled with some type of waste.

Time was trickling through his fingers as he searched. Frustration, fear, and anger mounted inside of Philip as he realized he didn't know this maze of tunnels and cells as well as he had hoped. His memory wasn't good enough to enable him to search the large expanse of this cave prison and find his fairy friend in time.

"We are running out of time!" He muttered in exasperation to Alayna, who was tight by his side. The sound of distant shouts from above told him that the guards were making their way closer as they moved lower through the levels of the prison.

She put a hand on his arm to pull him to a stop. "I think it's this way, Philip." And she set off in a different direction from the one in which they had been moving, without waiting for his response. She led them along an extremely narrow side corridor where the light almost failed them because of the lack of torches.

How did Alayna think she knew where to go? It made no sense. Yet, something told Philip to follow her and keep his mouth shut. It couldn't hurt. He hadn't been able to find Beathan yet and time was running out. Maybe she could succeed where he had failed.

She moved with assurance now. The longer she led it was as if she grew more certain of their path.

"Yes," she murmured, "it should be somewhere near here. We are almost there. I can feel it." What exactly could she feel, he wondered?

Finally, they rounded a rocky bend and came upon a cluster of jail cells. A dark shape huddled in one, and Philip couldn't tell what it was, only that it was weeping. The despondent sound of sobs and the shaking of the mound of flesh filled the dense air. The second cell was occupied by a witch—again muzzled—and an impish creature with which Philip wasn't familiar. Was it a type of goblin?

He looked into the third cell, the one to which Alayna was indicating, and he saw they had reached their destination. Beathan was sitting slumped against the wall with his hands shackled to the floor beside him. He was bleeding from the wrists, not effusively, but enough to make him groggy—or at least it appeared that way from the way his head lolled on his shoulders.

"Philip? Ya' came." The gypsy-fairy's voice sounded weak and tired but it still had a hint of mischief buried in it.

Philip grabbed the bars of the cell door and wrenched with every ounce of strength inside him. The grated door groaned and then the hinges burst from the strain, allowing Philip to rip the door free and drop it at his side to clatter in the darkness of the cave.

He stepped inside the cell and approached Beathan. "I came," he said simply.

"Would ya' look at that, ya've up and gone completely rogue on me now, haven't ya'? Engineerin' a prison break like this..." the fairy's joke made Philip smile. Even locked in a cell he was witty as ever.

"Not quite," Philip responded.

Philip appraised the situation, taking stock of the condition in which he found Beathan. He wouldn't be his usual self in a fight right now, weak as he was.

"Well, are ya' goin' to get me out o' these manacles?" The half-breed asked impatiently.

"So you want my help, do you?" Philip smirked, unable to pass up the opportunity to tease his friend.

"I'd not rightly word it so..." The fairy disputed with a weak laugh.

Alayna interrupted. "Boys, I'm not sure now is the time for jokes, or a contest of wills over who needs whom. Your pride can wait until later!"

"What a wise lass. I knew we saved her for a reason."

"And I owe you for that," Philip said, all joking aside now.

He grabbed the chains and ripped them from the ground. Beathan stood and grasped the chains that hung from the shackles around his wrists. The fairy half-breed hefted them, watching them swing.

"Not bad for a makeshift weapon, eh?" He suggested giving one chain a controlled swing.

"Not bad at all," Philip responded, "But I'm not sure you'll be up to fighting right now." He glanced down at Beathan's bloody wrists again. "What happened?"

Beathan grimaced as he saw where Philip was looking. "They've been bleedin' me on account o' the fact they view me as extra dangerous." The fairy winked as if it were all a big joke. "Nearly escaped on the way here an' they want t' keep me weak. They've also been fillin' me full o' herbs o' some sort. The kind that make me fuzzy in the head an' make it hard to remember me charms an' spells. Tis true, I'll likely not be of much use to ya' in a fight at the moment."

Philip tore two strips of cloth from the bottom of his shirt and made a makeshift bandage for the fairy's wrists. Hopefully that would stop the minor bleeding and allow Beathan to begin regaining his strength. The half-breed didn't have Philip's ability to heal precisely, but he did rebound from injury quicker than most. Hopefully, staunching the blood trickling from his arms would be enough to start the healing process.

Time was short, however, and overthinking would get them caught just as much as Beathan's weakness might. It was time to move. However, one last question pressed on Philip's mind, a question he had to ask.

"Alayna, I'm confused. How did you know how to find Beathan? You've never been here before." Philip turned away from his gypsy friend to face her as he spoke.

Alayna opened her mouth to speak, but before she could utter a word, a shape rustled in the darkness behind Philip and an accented, cultured voice answered his question.

"She did not find the fairy. She found me."

CHAPTER TWELVE

Instinctively Philip's hands checked his various weapons to be prepared for anything that might come next. That voice from the gloom on the other side of the cell had surprised him. Philip felt the knife and stake at his belt, as well as remembering the knives hidden in both of his boots—tools courtesy of Stephen's pilfering.

"Relax," the voice assured them in its urbane, eastern accent.

"Who are you?" Philip demanded harshly. He supposed he should have known Beathan would have a companion of sorts after the mental communication Alayna had received in Trondheim, but for some reason he hadn't figured that person into any of his plans.

Beathan answered Philip's question. "That's Azir. He'll be accompanyin' us out o' this fine place."

"As he said, I am Azir." The shape shifted and stood as it moved in their direction, becoming more visible as it came closer. He looked like one of the Elfas, but something was different, it was as if this Elfas was just a bit off somehow. Azir was darker in the eyes and hair, more hollow cheeked, and his pale skin had the faintest ashy complexion in comparison to the fairness of Alayna.

"Why is he in here?" Philip asked Beathan.

"Ill fortune, same as me." The fairy smiled as winningly as possible.

"Right," Philip snorted.

"Ya' cared not to ask why I was brought to this fine establishment."

The fairy indicated the jail around them as if it was a palace and he at his leisure. "Why do ya' need to know his reason for bein' here?"

"Because I'm not in debt to him." Philip said simply.

He eyed Azir again, but Philip still felt uncomfortable. He couldn't put a finger on what it was. The Elfas weren't known for being dangerous, but his gut told him not to free Azir, that he was a threat to him and Alayna.

"I don't know you and I don't trust you." Philip spoke bluntly.

"You simply must free me." Azir's voice acquired a silky edge and caressed Philip's mind. Everything told him to do as the voice said. Every fiber of his being screamed for him to release the prisoner across from Beathan. He resisted.

A moment passed before Azir repeated himself. "I said... You. Must. Free. Me." This time the force of the Elfas' mind hit Philip like a sledgehammer, all caressing gone. Realization hit Philip's mind simultaneously as he fended off the mental attack as best he could. He'd dealt with this many times while working as a Collector. His resolve firmed and he clung to his free will by the mental fingertips of his mind.

Alayna, however, hadn't the training that Philip had. She'd never been taught by the Guild to resist the persuasive mental faculties of a vampire and she was already reaching out towards the manacles as if she could somehow help Azir. Philip knew she couldn't do anything, she wasn't strong enough to rip the chains free, but reflexively he spoke anyway.

"No," he shouted at Alayna more firmly than he had intended. He shouted loudly enough that she was startled out of the half-trance into which the Elfas'—no the vampire's voice—had seduced her.

Confused, she looked at Philip. "What's happening? What is going on?" She put a hand to her head as if it ached.

"We will not be taking the likes of him with us when we go. I didn't come all this way for his kind." Philip spat out that last bit even as he answered her question indirectly. He hated vampires. There would be time to explain later. "But first Azir, were you... like this... when you contacted Alayna's mind?"

"Wouldn't you like to know?" Azir smirked at Philip. "I would imagine there might be all kinds of interesting effects if that were to prove to be the case."

Philip's teeth clenched in frustration. Alayna had been dragged into the middle of something new, something unknown. He was going to have a few choice words for Beathan later.

It was as if the half-fairy read his mind. "I know, Philip. I would never have had him do it had I known he was transitionin'." Beathan's voice carried sincere apology. It would have to do for now. They needed out of here.

The fairy continued. "I know ya' have values to hold to, Philip, but you're no longer one o' *them* an' ya' are not beholden to a code any more. Besides, I gave him my word that we would escape t'gether."

"One of them..." Azir speculated quietly to the side in a questioning manner. Philip could see his mind whirring like a machine as he tried to piece together what Beathan had meant by that comment.

"I don't care!" Philip exclaimed. "I'm not freeing him. His kind are dangerous and I don't owe him anything."

Alayna turned a quizzical eye to him. "What kind? We connected mind to mind, he must be one of my kind, the Elfas. We aren't dangerous, Philip. What are you talking about?"

"It is more complicated than that Alayna. He, isn't your kind any more, well not entirely that is."

Before Alayna could comment on that Azir interrupted their conversation. "That may be, but you need me. I have heard the bell tolling the alarm for quite some time now. The whole prison is alerted. You need my help to escape." Again he smirked with a self-satisfied, dark pleasure. Somehow, still chained, he managed to fill the cell with his presence in an imposing, almost regal fashion. If Philip had been an outsider looking into the cell, for all the world he would have thought the still-shackled Azir was the one in charge.

"'Tis true," Beathan spoke up. "Ya' cannot do it alone. Alayna, bless her, is not properly trained for combat, an' truly, I am weaker than I should be."

Philip ground his teeth again, giving in. Turning back to the vampire he said, "Fine. But let's get one thing straight. You need me as much as I need you. If I chose, we could all rot in here together. So I don't owe you any debt."

"Fine," Azir pursed his lips with a slightly sour expression, not liking to have the tables of the conversation turned on him. "We can agree that we are both helping the other for selfish reasons. Now, will you get me out of these ungainly contraptions?" He shook the manacles binding his wrists at Philip.

Philip grasped the chains and prepared to break them as he had Beathan's. But first one more thought crossed his mind. "Oh, one more thing, Azir, we aren't here to kill. Don't murder anyone unless there's no other alternative. Matter of fact, I don't care. If I see you kill even one person, I'll put you down! Got it? I have dealt with your kind before."

"Got your stake handy then?" Azir mocked Philip.

Alayna was still confused. "What are you talking about, Philip? I thought you said you never killed and hunted Alderfolk. He's an Elfas like me."

Philip ignored Alayna, not wanting to burden her with the truth and all the worries that would follow when she realized her mind had been invaded by a vampire.

Who knew what the consequences of that interaction would be? But there was time enough for those thoughts later, if they could escape. He furrowed his brow, and stared at the vampire until finally Azir conceded, hands raised slightly in defense as if he had never considered doing any such thing. "Of course... Collector. I will not kill any of your comrades up there." So the vampire had figured out what Beathan had meant by *them*. Oh, well, it wasn't as if it was a secret. He just wasn't sure he was keen on the vampire knowing his past and personal business.

"Philip, answer me!" Alayna's voice rang out demandingly. She didn't like being ignored.

"You will have to trust me, love. There's just no time to explain it all right now."

"No, I want to know now." Alayna was firm and decisive with her words. "He is an Elfas, why don't you trust him?" Before Philip could answer Azir responded for him.

"*Was*, pretty one. I was an Elfas." The vampire opened his mouth and licked a pure white fang suggestively. "But let us just say, I like to dabble in things more mysterious. Now, I am an outcast from our people and oh so much more than that."

Philip saw Alayna cringe and then shudder as she finally understood what was going on. Grabbing the chains in his hands, he twisted, shattering the links just below the metal cuffs.

Azir flashed a sly, toothy, white smile at Philip. Then in a blur of motion the vampire sprang towards him with more speed than Philip would have thought possible and buried his teeth in Philip's exposed neck.

———

He'd been bitten before—many times. He was used to the pain, the savage clamp of the jaws around his flesh, but there was something shameful in having it done to him right in front of Alayna. Philip was hardly defenseless, but he still didn't like Alayna seeing him being taken advantage of like this.

He felt his blood gushing into Azir's mouth as he grasped the vampire and yanked him away as hard as he could and then flung him against the stone of the wall on the other side of the cell. The vampire fell and then popped back up in rather spritely fashion for someone who had been imprisoned for weeks. Philip's blood must have done the vampire good.

"My first feeding." Azir supplied unasked information, wiping a rivulet of blood from his chin. "And I am so glad it was an unwilling victim. There is something so... freeing in my new nature—a power in the taking." He flexed his hands as if feeling a new vigor.

Philip stalked toward him with a stake, ready to kill the vampire for attacking him. However, the vampire had other ideas.

"Easy, Collector, I wouldn't have killed you."

"Like you could have," Philip sneered defiantly.

Azir ignored the comment and continued. "I fed on you to make sure I am strong enough to help us fight our way out of here and escape. They have been depriving me of blood, of my energy source. In order to hold up my end of the bargain, it was necessary." He licked his lips again, "Although, it was also quite satisfactory." He leered, a wicked grin in the flickering light.

Still Philip closed the distance while the vampire stood nonchalantly waiting. "You thought feeding on me was the way to repay me for freeing you?"

"Well, it was either you or the lass. Even though she looks an infinitely more tasty and tempting morsel, I figured you would have apoplexy if I bit her."

Philip stopped and pursed his lips as if sucking on something sour. This distraction was too much. He had to let it go for now and deal with it later.

Turning, he shoved aside his anger and barked, "Let's go," and headed for the cell of the door followed by Beathan and Alayna and the vampire's mocking laughter.

The prison was a riot of sounds. As Philip and his companions left the cell and started back the way they had come, the shouts and calls of guards mingled with the tolling of the alarm bell. Wailing arose from many of the rocky prisons along the way as if the prisoners—whether of sane mind or not—recognized that something was afoot and wanted to contribute to the mayhem in some way, even if that way was just to add to the noise. Philip decided the extra noise was a benefit, since it spread throughout the expanse of the prison and therefore wouldn't pinpoint their location.

He pulled a knife from his boot and offered it to Beathan. The fairy shook him off however, and hefted the short length of chains still hanging from the manacles on his wrists. Apparently he was satisfied with the makeshift weapons. Philip stuck the knife back in his boot and kept a hand near his belt, both to be near his own knife but also to be near the stake.

He felt a tingling sensation in his shoulder blades, the uncomfortable feeling of knowing that a bloodthirsty predator was just at his back, lusting after his blood. Philip put a hand to his neck to check the wound. It wasn't dire. After all, Azir didn't strike him as a foolish person—the vampire knew he needed Philip to help escape. But the wound still ached and burned, causing Philip annoyance. He hated entering a fight already wounded. It seemed like a bad omen.

They pushed onwards, trying to retrace his and Alayna's steps from earlier. However, what they ended up doing more than anything else was listening. Philip, leading the way, would pause for a moment at every intersection to listen. Down some paths he heard the noise of roving bands of Guild guards, traveling in small packs and searching for the intruders. Down other narrow, stony corridors Philip heard nothing and those silences directed their path. Before long it became clear they were hopelessly lost. He had no idea where they were, where the drainage chute back to the ocean was, or how to get there. It was time for a new plan.

He stopped. This wasn't a decision to make by himself. Philip turned to the group. Before he could speak the eastern Elfas and newly turned vampire spoke. "You are hopelessly lost, Collector, are you not?" The vampire asked in a smug voice that Philip found insufferable.

Philip tried to think if there was a way to avoid admitting it but couldn't. "Yes. It has been years since I was this far down into the lower levels of St. Thomas and I cannot find my way back to our entry point."

The vampire snickered at his response. He deliberately kept it hidden what their entry point had been. If they were not going to exit the same way, then he wanted to make sure the vampire didn't know about the secret, rocky pipeline to the ocean. Philip might not be a Collector any longer, and he was certainly not fully aligned in his mind and heart with the policies and practices of the Guild, but he still couldn't fully disapprove of what they did.

Many of the prisoners here in St. Thomas's were deadly and a plague on the entire world, the supernatural and humanity alike, and Philip would not condone the spread of information that might lead to the weakening of this prison. Not just yet. He supposed a part of him still felt like a Guild member, even though that part was small and buried deeply within him now.

"We have a decision to make. We can keep wandering around this bottom level indefinitely, or we can follow any one of the various pathways that lead up and try to make our escape that way." Philip laid out the two options evenly, calmly, then said, "I favor the latter."

"Fight our way out the front gate?" Alayna asked incredulously. Philip nodded and made a regretful face.

Beathan sighed gustily but then put on a good face. "'Twas bound t' come t' that, no?" He leaned against the wall as he spoke exuding a nonchalant fatalism. Only Beathan could manage that attitude and appearance in the midst of such a dire situation.

"So we go up." Azir put in his opinion. It wasn't a question. Philip didn't like the fact that the vampire spoke so decisively, but he was forced to agree since the vampire had settled upon the option which Philip, himself, proposed.

They all shared a somber look then Beathan shrugged, and Philip, Alayna, and Azir all nodded to let the others know they were in accord. Course set, Philip began picking paths not just to avoid the sound of pursuit, but also those that angled upwards slightly. They made their way, ascending steadily. Their path was not uncontested.

Around one corner they almost ran into a rather silent group of guard Collectors and were forced to fight. As tired and drained as he was, Beathan was the first to react. His instincts and reflexes had always been sharpest. Lightning quick, he whipped the links of chain in his hands and shattered the kneecap of one guard, incapacitating him, while Philip closed the distance on another. Philip engaged and practically clubbed the man in the face with his hard, battle-worn, brawler's fists. The calluses kept Philip's knuckles safe from serious harm. The guard dropped like a pile of firewood, collected and then discarded. Philip heard the sounds of a scuffle around him and saw the lithe frame of

Alayna ducking and dancing around her opponent until she managed to drop him with a swift, high kick to the temple. She might not be the experienced fighter that Beathan and Philip were but she held her own well. Azir similarly acquitted himself, easily disposing of the guard he faced in a rushing attack to the man's neck.

"Azir" Beathan reprimanded his prison companion, and the vampire stopped feeding and let the guard slump to the stone floor unconscious.

"I said no killing," Philip's hand was already reaching for his wooden stake in anger.

Azir turned and grinned with pleasure, wiping blood from his face with the back of his hand.

"Have you no faith in my self-restraint?" He asked rhetorically before continuing. "It was just a quick drink, enough to put him to sleep, but barely enough to do him any lasting harm. Do not worry, Collector, your comrade will be perfectly fine."

"He's not my comrade," Philip protested in annoyance.

"Whatever you say," Azir politely disagreed in an affable way, flashing a strange look at Alayna while he did so. However, Alayna didn't seem to be paying attention, she was peering down the corridor, alert and waiting to move on.

And so they made their way up. Through the levels of the prison they fought small bands of Collectors in twos and threes, avoiding them when they could but giving battle when they couldn't. Once they saw a group of hulking, nonhuman shapes shambling in another direction of the dim, mazelike interior. Deadbloods. Philip shuddered as he thought of the somewhat-dead creatures under the control of the Blood Mages. It was not long before Philip recognized that they were reaching the uppermost level of the prison. Soon they would be approaching the ground level of the building. Trepidation filled him. It had been too easy.

They left the last ascending corridor and stepped through a real doorframe onto wood plank floors. They were in the building proper now.

"Here we are," Beathan gestured expansively to their new surroundings. It was the inside of the monastery structure and they were close to finding their escape.

"Easier than I thought it would be," the fairy murmured, echoing Philip's thoughts.

"Too easy." Philip's agreement was nervous, cautious. There should have been more guards, more Deadbloods, something more.

They turned a corner and entered a large, empty room, an entertaining room to be filled or emptied at the owner's desire and it all became clear. Light shone through stain glass windows high on the walls, shooting down in colored rays and streamers to illuminate their opposition. Ahead of them waited two massively hulking Minotaurs—Deadbloods for sure—eyeing them with blankly focused expressions.

"Philip...?" Alayna said questioningly.

Philip turned to look behind them, about to counsel that they run from the powerful and Blood-Mage-controlled beasts while they could, but as he did, ten Collectors filtered into the room from behind them, effectively closing off their escape route. It was a trap. The only way out was to fight.

Philip waited for the ten guards to close the distance and engage them, but instead they sat back, waiting. Of course, the light dawned in his mind. The Collectors would wait and let the Deadbloods do the work for them and clean up the mess afterwards if it was needed. Why bloody their hands when they could use their pet monsters to do it instead. As if on cue, the two Minotaurs advanced.

Philip had never faced a Minotaur. They were uncommon in most of Europe and unheard of in the New World. They often preferred to stay in their home region of Greece and even more specifically, frequenting the wilds and gorges of the Isle of Crete.

He realized, in facing these two monsters, that he was woefully inexperienced and drastically undersized. They marched forward, each about seven and a half feet tall. Not so tall as the troll he had faced in the mountains of Norway, but he had been lucky to temporarily vanquish that troll. Besides, these two carried weapons, making the conflict likely to be infinitely more dangerous and challenging. One of the Deadblood Minotaurs stepped forward on cloven feet, giving way to the legs and torso of a giant man, until lastly becoming the head of a bull. Its horns spiraling off the sides of its bovine head were intimidating, but not nearly as much as the wickedly curved scimitar that it carried. The other Minotaur, walked on human feet, with a humanoid body that gave way to a bull's face as well, although its horns were smaller and blunted as if they had been chopped off—maybe in punishment at some point. It wielded a giant, battle-axe and advanced with a menacing stride.

Philip stepped forward to engage the one with the battle-axe. "I'll take this one since I'm healthiest and most able of all of us. You three work together on the other." It was madness to think he could face this Deadblood alone, wasn't it? But there was no other option.

Beathan appeared drained and exhausted, Alayna was holding her own for the most part, but she was not trained for combat such as this, and the vampire, well the vampire was an unknown. Who knew how much fighting experience he really had? It would likely take three of them to bring that one down. Hopefully, Philip would be able to occupy this one long enough for them to make their escape.

To her credit, Alayna only spared one worried glance at him before acquiescing to his request. She knew her strengths and weaknesses and she knew his. Philip was the authority in a situation like this.

Philip focused on the Deadblood Minotaur before him. He had to get inside its defenses to engage a close fight, much like he had with the troll. However, as the beast swung an arching, horizontal blow with its battle-axe, Philip was forced back and realized that it would be more difficult than he had anticipated.

He spared a glance at the other three who had spread themselves around the other Deadblood in a triangle. Philip couldn't watch his companions any longer as the battle-axe careened in his direction again and he was forced to dive to avoid it, but he knew his companions' tactics would have to be wolf-like. Pack mentality to bring down a larger more dangerous foe.

The battle-axe collided with the floor, spraying shards of splintered wood, right where Philip had been standing before he dove. In a roll, Philip closed the distance with his opponent and began hammering his fists with powerful blows into the midsection of the Deadblood. His troll-blood-infused strength would hopefully be enough to cause this Deadblood pause. The beast fought in eerie silence, grunting with effort occasionally but emitting no other sounds. It swiped a blow at Philip and caught him with the flat of the axe, stunning him slightly.

Philip flew backwards a few feet from the blow, landing on his back. Vaguely, he heard the sounds of his companions fighting. There was the clinking of Beathan's two makeshift chain maces, the patter of Alayna's lithe feet as she danced in and out of range to strike, and the sick tearing sound of flesh. Hamstring tearing. Philip knew that sound. The vampire's predatory instincts must have helped it identify a weakness. Perhaps Azir was using one of Alayna's knives to rip through their opponent's muscle to cripple it.

All those sounds he heard and categorized in a brief moment before

Philip was hard pressed to avoid his own defeat. The battle-axe swung down as the beast stomped forwards, and he rolled one way to avoid the killing blow. He stood up as quickly as he could after avoiding it.

The battle-axe was caught in the floor, hooked on some unseen obstacle. Without a thought the Deadblood let it go and drew what looked like a knife from its belt, although to Philip, it was more like a short sword. It swung the blade, its bare chest rippling with hard, toned muscles. Philip dodged once but then the return strike flashed across his chest and he felt the slice of a blade scouring his body. It wasn't a deep wound, fortunately, but Philip felt the blood begin to flow freely and drip steadily onto the wooden floor at his feet.

His heart sank, not just because of the detriment of the wound to his fighting ability, but also for what it signified should he escape this encounter. The Blood Mages would find the residue of his blood from this fight very convenient. There was no time to wallow in disappointment however, as he dodged again to avoid a killing swipe of the sword at his head.

The Minotaur was fast, but not lightning quick. However, it was a skilled weapon wielder—uncommon in many supernatural creatures—and Philip needed to end this fight.

He felt the burning of his wounded chest join with the pain of some of his fresh scars from the fight in Liverpool tearing open. His faded, sleeveless tunic was stained red with blood. Philip closed the distance again and managed to get inside the stroke of the sword. He pulled a knife and jammed it into the thigh of the creature before following up the strike with a few harsh blows of his fist. Finally, Philip struck a blow directly into the knee of the beast and he felt bone shatter. The Minotaur didn't scream—Deadbloods were an odd sort—but it did crumple slightly. Classic tactics. When your opponent outsized you, and outweighed you then you had to incapacitate it. Make it unable to carry its own weight. That usually meant attacking its legs and feet.

As a follow up, Philip pulled his knife from the beast's thigh and plunged it into the Minotaur's foot on its uninjured leg, all the while avoiding another swing of the sword. Philip danced back out of range, and he watched as the beast tried to hobble forwards but instead collapsed, unable to bear its weight and continue the fight. Satisfied, he turned in fear for his companions only to see a dead Minotaur at their feet.

They must have hobbled it together, similar to his tactics, and then made quick work of it while it was on the ground. There was no time to waste however, as the guards began advancing without a word as soon as it was clear the Deadbloods were defeated. One Minotaur was dead, and Philip's opponent wouldn't be fighting any time soon, so now it was up to the Collectors to finish the job. The rearguard of Collectors moved towards them.

Beathan turned a questioning eye towards Philip as the ten Collectors advanced carefully. "Run?" the half-fairy asked.

"Run," Philip agreed and the four of them sprinted for the door that the Deadbloods had been blocking. It was likely futile. They were tired, winded from the fight, from imprisonment, and from long journeys, but Philip was out of ideas. They would probably have to turn and fight eventually but for now they would run. They charged through a few empty rooms until they reached the gateway out of the monastery. Philip heard the shouts of the Collectors as they followed.

Philip, Alayna, Beathan, and Azir burst through the large wooden door and into the sunlight of the courtyard. Beathan was looking faint, and Azir was even paler than normal as well, as if he had expended enough energy that he needed another drink to replenish his inner fuel. Philip's wound was burning and still bleeding freely, as were the older wounds that had split open. Of them all, only Alayna looked like she was in any shape to make an escape.

"It's no use," Philip panted as they ran out of the courtyard, through the gateway, and onto the free soil outside the prison boundaries.

The guards following them had easily caught up. Philip called his companions to a halt. They would have to face this threat head on.

"Fleein' was long odds to work anyhow," Beathan shrugged his acceptance at the necessity of a fight after all, as if he had hardly a care in the world. Yet the drawn creases around his eyes spoke otherwise.

"Again we fight." Azir looked pale but a feverish light seemed to gleam in his eyes as he gazed upon the Collectors that had arrayed themselves around Philip and the group of escapees.

"I wish I had my crossbow," was all Alayna said. Squaring up to fight.

They were a brave bunch, Philip had to admit.

The Collectors closed in with their fighting tactics. Two or three guards for each of them. Philip took the fight to them. He smashed his fist in the face of the first guard to come within his reach, sending the man reeling while another took his place.

Three Collectors with stakes closed in on Azir and Philip saw an expression of fear on the vampire's face as he watched the wooden weapons in the hands of the men approaching him. Yet he fought tenaciously, avoiding the swings of the stakes and sinking his teeth into any exposed flesh he could. Philip saw him tear out the throat of one Collector viciously. Men were going to die today. Philip had hoped it would not be the case, but there was no avoiding it now.

Two more guards attacked Philip and he felt a crossbow bolt of a small size, like Alayna's, bury itself in his shoulder. He ripped it out and flung it at one attacker, the bolt clattering into the man's face with its blunt end. The other guard was more cautious. He held a hand axe and a narrow dueling sword in either hand, weaving them in a menacing fashion.

The guard facing Philip whipped his rapier-like blade, which flicked a new cut on Philip's arm. Then he slashed again opening up a cut on Philip's leg. Philip yanked the stake from his belt. It wasn't the ideal weapon but it was the one that came to his hand first. He threw it with practiced aim. The wooden weapon was not specially crafted to be used against humans, but it was hard and sharp. The stake flew from Philip's hand and sunk into the man's stomach with a sickening thud.

The Collector dropped to his knees on the muddy grass and his eyes glazed over in the pre-death shock that often occurred to victims that were casualties of battle. A breeze gusted up off the ocean and over the cliff's edge carrying the cloying scent of blood to Philip's nostrils. He almost gagged. He hated killing humans.

The others of his companions fared differently. Azir, like Philip, had dispatched his opponents in typically bloody fashion, leaving a wake of torn throats. He had gone to the aid of the hard-pressed Alayna. The two of them stood back to back, fighting in unison as if they had done it all their lives. For a second, Philip felt a surge of jealousy at the sight, an emotion compounded by the fact that as they dispatched their two opponents, Alayna turned her face and flashed a quick, fierce grin to the vampire. Immediately after realizing what she had done, her face smoothed back into a mask of calmness. However, Philip knew her well and could see uncertainty flickering under that mask.

It was Beathan, however, who was not doing well. Three guards had flanked him, only kept at bay by the exhausted flailing of the fairy's makeshift chain maces. The half-gypsy would not be able to hold out much longer. A small crossbow bolt was plunged into his thigh and a guard was aiming another bolt at his chest. Philip picked up a rock and threw it at the man with the crossbow. It struck him just as he fired, and the bolt went askew, streaking past Beathan's head and over the cliff to fall out of sight into the grey-blue beyond.

The four of them now attacked the remaining Collectors with the odds in their favor. Even in their weakened state they made quick work of the few Collectors who were left, taking them down in a flurry of blows.

Philip still felt the energy from the fight keeping him upright but a flicker of amazement tickled his mind. Perhaps he and his companions had avoided the better fighters that had been sent below at the sounding of the alarm bell and this rearguard of Collectors was not as experienced.

If so, he and his companions had been lucky. A little fortune was always necessary to accomplish the unthinkable. And they were on course to do just that. They hadn't completed their escape yet, there would still be pursuit, but they were en route to do what had never been done—break into St. Thomas's and free captives. However, Philip had been in the Guild his whole life. He knew there was more to come. The prison had defenses they had yet to face. Soon the Haunts would be released, if they had not been already. It was time to run again.

CHAPTER THIRTEEN

"Who would've thought we'd survive?" Beathan quipped with a weak grin. "Maybe that palace o' a prison is not quite the impregnable chunk o' rock everyone says. Not all reputations measure up." He placed a hand on his chest to indicate that, of course, his own reputation did.

Philip shook his head as they gathered themselves. "Wipe that smile off your face, Beathan. This isn't over yet."

As if it had been easy. All four of them featured blood and wounds from fighting their way out of St. Thomas's. Philip especially was covered with injuries.

The half fairy tilted his head in question as he rested his hands on his knees and panted. Alayna and Azir perked their heads in attention also.

Philip continued. He might as well tell them. "There will be more Deadbloods on our trail soon. A specific type called the Haunts. They are creatures that guard the area surrounding the prison. They'll be recalled by the mages, if they have not been already. As soon as they return, they'll set out in pursuit of us. There is no time to waste, we have to move now."

As he spoke he picked up a thin sword used by one of the dead Collectors. Philip wasn't much for formal weapons, preferring his fists and maybe a small blade or a stake, but he knew his way around a sword from his years of training and something told him the better armed they were the more chance they had of surviving.

Everyone was exhausted and drained, but from their expressions, they knew the truth of what Philip said. If they could cover just a few leagues of distance, they could reach the cove where their ship was waiting. Once aboard, their escape would be complete.

They set out at a steady run, but Philip knew they wouldn't be able to hold the pace for long. He healed faster than a normal man but his recovery still took time. His body screamed for rest and for his wounds to be bandaged, but there was nothing to do but run.

His companions were not faring much better. Beathan, having been bled for days and fed drugs in the cell looked to be on the verge of collapse every step he took. Alayna was a runner, her kind was bred to cover distance quickly, but she was not used to the exertions of combat, and her feet plodded more than they usually did. He could see the drawn weariness in her eyes and she carried no few injuries herself, although fortunately most of them looked shallow. Yet, superficial wounds, when untreated, could still lead to collapse and then death.

Of all of them, Azir seemed to retain the most vigor. However, Philip knew that as a vampire he would require blood soon to replenish the power and energy he'd used while fighting in the escape. It wouldn't be long before he began to lag also, and when he did, he would start looking for blood. It was his nature. Philip kept a close eye on Azir as they staggered on as fast as they could.

"So what are these Haunts precisely? Do you mean to say you believe in ghosts? That our spirits somehow walk the earth when we are gone?" Azir asked, and then ended the statement with just a hint of a sneer.

"Not ghosts or spirits exactly," Philip replied wearily, panting and sweating as he ran. "But they do have some of the capabilities attributed to ghosts. Namely the ability to materialize and dematerialize at will."

All three of his companions whipped their heads around in surprise at that statement. He supposed it was rather confounding. The power to dematerialize was not one he had heard of in any supernatural creatures apart from the Haunts. A touch of fear clouded their eyes as they listened to him. Good. They should be afraid. There was a reason the Haunts were set to protect the land around St. Thomas's.

"They are nearly impossible to fight, since every time you attempt to strike a blow they vanish and your weapon only flies through the air in which they previously stood." Philip didn't want to sweeten this for them. "We do not want to face them. They make short work of everyone they come across. Our best chance is to outdistance them. They are

Deadbloods and require the mages to work their craft on their blood and keep them alive. Once a day this can be done. Like all Deadbloods, the Haunts will only be able to travel about a half day's journey away from their Blood Mage masters before they will be forced to return, or risk death."

"Good thing we have a ship awaiting us then, is it not?" Azir cocked his head toward Philip with a searching look. It was almost as if he questioned whether or not that was true.

They ran for an hour or so, until they reached the bluff overlooking the cove in which Philip had directed Dimsby and his ship to await them. Philip had sailed this coastline many times during his years as a Collector, and he was more familiar with it than most places in the world. This cove a was secluded inlet of water, safe from prying eyes. It was the perfect place to drop anchor and wait for a day. Or at least it would have been.

Philip's heart dropped as he looked out over the water from atop the cliff. No ship was waiting for them. The steep, stony path leading down from the top of the bluff to the shore's edge would be challenging in their injured condition, and there was no point in even attempting it. The sly captain had broken his promise to Philip and Alayna.

He supposed that the easy fare provided to carry them from Liverpool to St. Thomas's hadn't been sufficient to get the man to hold his ship for them one day. It was a major set back. How were they to escape now? The next town would take them nearly a day to reach in their weakened, injured state, and even if they did reach the small port, he had no guarantee that a ship would be waiting in harbor and ready to set sail at their convenience.

"Do my eyes deceive me, or is this cove empty of all but wind and waves?" Azir sneered ever so slightly as he spoke. Despite the imposition the situation caused to his own escape, the vampire clearly was finding some measure of enjoyment from the fact that Philip's plan and claim of a ship to be waiting for them had gone awry. Philip couldn't figure out why the vampire hated him so. Although, he had to admit the feeling was mutual. Perhaps it was Philip's past as a Collector. Most supernatural beings found it hard to reconcile their differences with anyone who had any association with the Guild.

Or perhaps the vampire's dislike stemmed from something else Philip thought as he glanced at Alayna. Azir was standing unnecessarily close to her and saying something in a low voice. The wind was whipping off the

MATHIAS G. B. COLWELL

ocean and it smothered Azir's words, carrying them away before Philip could hear what the vampire was saying.

He narrowed his eyes as the green of envy slithered its way into his heart. Alayna looked uncomfortable with the part Elfas, part vampire's mouth so close to her ear, yet she didn't pull away immediately as Philip would have expected. At least, she didn't end the close proximity between her and Azir until she noticed Philip watching them.

Philip opened his mouth to say something when out of nowhere another Alayna appeared some distance away. The new Alayna was walking towards them with the confidence and assurance only a supreme predator can achieve.

The Haunts had arrived.

CHAPTER FOURTEEN

Beathan breathed deeply of the fresh, tangy air whipping up off the water and onto the bluff. His body trembled with exhaustion and blood loss. No way around it. He hadn't been this tired since the time he'd spent nearly a month with that Siren in the Aegean. What a wondrous few weeks that had been. And he'd managed to escape the beautiful and deadly sea witch with his mind and body intact, so survival had been a plus as well. He smiled briefly at the memory of her lustrous, salty hair. She had been worth the risk, and the exhaustion.

This, on the other hand, Beathan could do without. He hoped to never be imprisoned again. Perhaps he should give up his thieving ways once and for all. If he did so, then he needn't worry about being pursued and possibly captured again. What a ludicrous thought! He snickered. He might as well give up breathing as stop being who he was—a scoundrel and mischief-maker, with a reputation for chicanery to uphold. Freedom came with a price.

His thoughts were interrupted by Philip's shout of surprise. Beathan turned away from the watery expanse of horizon and looked behind him. Alayna was walking along the path towards them. No wait. Alayna was standing next to Azir. Wait, why were Alayna and Azir so close to one another? Beathan shook his head to clear his thoughts. Alayna and Azir's proximity were hardly what was important at the moment. The real question was, why was there a second Alayna?

"Philip, mate, what's happenin'?" Beathan asked uncertainly. Something told him this was seriously wrong.

Philip swore angrily. "I should have expected them to catch us quickly."

"Who are they? I only see one." Azir asked, echoing Beathan's thoughts exactly.

"What am I doing over there? What is going on?" Alayna was just as confused as the rest of them. Only Philip seemed to understand why there were two Alayna's and what it meant. Judging by the look on his face, it meant nothing good.

"It's the Haunts. I didn't get a chance to explain everything to you before." Philip spoke hurriedly as the other Alayna slowly closed the distance between them. "I was hoping to avoid them entirely, since they patrol the land around St. Thomas's but our ship captain double-crossed us, and the Blood Mages must have recalled them to the monastery as soon as we broke free. They are faster than I thought."

"Mate, I think ya' need to tell us more about these creatures," Beathan said with unexpected trepidation. He wasn't often scared, and certainly never because of something so trivial as a terrifying beast. Yet Beathan had just spied another figure walking toward them from another direction. This figure made his blood run cold. Beathan saw himself strutting towards them with the insolent swagger that he knew only he himself possessed. It was like looking in a moving mirror—a horribly accurate, living reflection of himself.

"Explanations can wait," Philip stated seriously. "We can talk later—if we survive." Philip squared his shoulders to fight.

As Beathan watched the Haunts approach, an idea began to form. Beathan knew that he and his companions needed rest. They were in no condition to fight. Perhaps he had a trick up his sleeve that could help. Idly he fiddled with the newest ring he had stolen, the one that possessed the defensive charm. He had discovered the beginning of its capabilities in the cell, when he had uttered the general, catch-all spell to activate its ability. The test had stopped the water from dripping onto him from the ceiling above him. Maybe he could make the spell even stronger this time. It would be a hurried and unexplored attempt at magic, but what else could he do? He was in no condition to help them fight. But maybe he could do this one thing.

"Quickly, everyone close to me!" He barked the order with more command than he had meant. It got everyone's attention. Azir looked like he was about to argue, contrary as he was, but Philip took one look at Beathan's face and agreed.

"Do what he says." Philip commanded.

Beathan felt an unusual flush of appreciation for Philip's trust in him. Nobody else trusted him. And with good reason. He took what he wanted, when he wanted, and pretty much thought of only himself. Yet, for some reason, the one-time Collector had faith in Beathan's judgment.

The four of them gathered together back to back as the duplicate Alayna and Beathan strode closer. They were only a stone's throw away now, advancing steadily through the short grass and moss. The other Beathan looked identical to him, all except for the eyes. There was something tellingly different—almost blank, dead-like—in the way they gazed at the one they were mimicking.

Beathan knew he didn't have much time. He thought quickly. The general spell he had used in the cell had revealed the charm as a defensive charm. Beathan wracked his brain, trying to remember any defensive spells that might work with his new charm ring. Finally, a spell came to mind. He thought it would work, he just had to execute it before their pursuers closed the distance completely.

With a quick breath, he uttered the defensive charm, hoping it would work. He flicked his ring as he channeled the magical ability into the charmed piece of jewelry. Now what? Beathan didn't know how to test it before the time when it would be needed, which was now!

"Well?" Philip asked.

"Well, what?" Beathan quipped back, never one to let the possibility to poke fun at his friend slip by.

Philip rolled his eyes in exasperation. "You know what. Did it work?"

"Oh, that?" Beathan grinned. "Don't rightly know. We'll discover the answer t' that question in a moment though." He indicated the two Haunts who were now almost within touching distance.

All four of them squared up to fight. Philip grasped a sword that he had lifted from the body of one of the dead guards. Alayna had a knife in one hand and Azir stood loose and ready, fangs bared, and nails that were not quite claws, ready to slash at his foes. None of them knew whether Beathan's charm had worked. Neither did he. The only thing to do was wait and see.

The Haunts came to within three feet of Beathan before they hit an invisible barrier of some kind. The defensive charm had worked. Beathan felt a shock go through his mind and body as the Haunts struck his magical wall. It was like a mental blow that reverberated down through his body all the way out to his fingers and toes. It wasn't painful exactly, but something told him that he wouldn't be able to withstand its force forever. The Haunts backed away and then circled, testing the invisible barrier that was erected in a circle around the four companions. The creatures didn't speak, they just prowled, testing, waiting.

Beathan and his companions stood nervously, watching the Haunts explore the magical barrier. Before long two more Haunts joined them, this time in the form of Philip and Azir. It was a surreal experience for the four of them to witness the replicas of themselves with their dead eyes stalking around them only a few feet away.

The Haunts tilted their heads every so often as if they couldn't understand what was happening, what was preventing them from attacking their prey. Yet their lack of understanding didn't lead them to frustration or anger, like many supernatural beasts. Instead, the Haunts just calmly and persistently tested the barrier again and again, sending shock waves through Beathan's mind and body at each attempt to breach the invisible wall.

"Philip, I think you had better tell us more about these Haunts while we have a moment of respite." Alayna's voice feigned calm, but Beathan could hear that underneath the serenity, she'd been rattled by the eerie confrontation with herself. They all were. Seeing a living-breathing version of yourself would do that to you.

Philip nodded reluctantly. "The Haunts are a group of Deadbloods who patrol the land surrounding the monastery and keep unwelcome visitors away. Like us, only we were able to circumvent their patrols."

"Yes, yes you said that already, Collector." Azir's voice was silky and smooth now. Beathan didn't think anyone could mistake it for anything other than what it was—the voice of a crooning predator.

Philip ignored the vampire's jibe. "They can only receive the magic of the Blood Mages, which staves off their death, once a day. Too much magic and they die, too little and they die.

Once a day the Blood Mages work their magic and give life to the blood within the Haunts' veins, enough for them to last a day without another magical transfusion. I explain this so that you, Beathan, realize that you only need to hold this barrier a few hours at most before the Haunts will need to leave us to return to their magical captors who hold the key to their survival.

We traveled some distance from St. Thomas's already, and if the

Haunts hope to survive, then they will not be able to stay here and circle this barrier forever. They will have to return to the Blood Mages sooner than later. Then we can run again."

Beathan wiped a bead of sweat building on his forehead. It was already growing difficult to hold the spell. He gritted his teeth and set his will. He wasn't about to be captured or killed by some mockery version of himself. There was only one half-fairy, half-gypsy named Beathan and it was him. He would walk away from this place alive.

"Why do they look like us?" Alayna's question was muted, no doubt due to the disconcerting activity of watching yourself and the one you loved prowling around you in a circle, waiting to attack.

"I do not know the specifics of it. All I know is that the Haunts form some kind of psychic connection with their quarry, their prey. And because they are not bound by the same laws of nature as we—they can dematerialize their physical form at will—this enables them to assume the form of those they hunt. I do not know what their true shape is, or even if they have one."

"This psychic connection, what else does it entail?" Azir was keen to understand the details. After hearing why he had chosen the life of a vampire—partially for the experiment of seeing what would happen—Beathan almost imagined he could hear the scientific whirring of Azir's mind.

"I do not know the full extent." Philip answered. "But, I do know that although they can assume the form of their prey, they cannot assume the supernatural physical capabilities of the creature they hunt. However, they can nevertheless, assimilate much of the mental activity of their prey due to their psychic connection. This means that a well-trained soldier or warrior would face a Haunt who not only looked like them but could also fight with the training and skill equal to theirs.

So, Vampire, your Haunt double does not have your silken voice or the venom to turn a person into a vampire, but because your predatory instinct is a predominantly mental faculty, almost a primal training your brain receives upon its transition, the Haunt that looks like you will be able to fight in the same way—pinpointing the weak spots of its opponents. Its mental connection with you will afford it some of your mental attributes."

Beathan shuddered as he imagined one of the Haunts being able to replicate a quarry to the extent that it mimicked their supernaturally physical traits in addition to gaining access to their minds. The mental aspect was horrible enough, but at least the Haunt that looked like Philip would not have his strength. It would have his combat training, but it would not fight with the power he did. Yet its own, personal ability to materialize and dematerialize at will would more than make up for that, no doubt.

"They will not give up, not until their masters, the Blood Mages, tell them they can. As soon as they leave, we must flee again and hope to reach the nearest port. With luck there may be a ship in port which can give us passage." Philip finished his explanation of their supernatural attackers.

The other Azir stepped forward and walked into the barrier, sending a familiar shockwave through Beathan. For a moment Beathan felt weak, as if he wouldn't be able to hold the spell, but then he drew deeply upon the well of strength within him and firmed up the invisible wall again. Yet, there was no denying, he was losing strength. He just had to outlast the magic of the Blood Mages. The Deadbloods would have to leave soon, Philip had said, in order to return to their masters so that they could survive another day. Idly, Beathan mused that he would rather be dead than on such a short leash as the Haunts. Well, any leash at all, no matter the length, was insufferable.

The Haunts prowled in silence, occasionally testing the barrier. An hour went by. This time it was Beathan and his companions who mimicked the others, in that none of them spoke and in doing so replicated the silence of the Haunts. The only exception to this quiet was when Azir mentioned how handsome he was, while cocking his head and gazing at the other him. One would think he was preening the way he gazed at the replica of himself, so proud was he of his elegant, if slightly too thin, appearance.

Another hour passed and the afternoon set in. They had to leave soon, didn't they? Beathan didn't know how much longer he could last. Finally, as one, the four replicas turned and loped off to the west along the cliff-top path towards St. Thomas's. It would take the creatures until almost morning to get back, judging by the distance Beathan and his companions had covered before their arrival.

After a suitably cautious amount of time, Beathan, at Philip's direction, allowed the defensive charm to cease and the barrier to drop. Beathan sagged to the soil in exhaustion.

Philip put a hand on Beathan's shoulder in thanks and Alayna smiled her quiet approval of his effort to protect them. Only Azir grinned a bit sardonically at Beathan, as if unimpressed with the fairy's effort. Vampire bastard! Beathan thought with uncharacteristic prejudice. Azir wouldn't say a word of thanks if his life depended on it.

"I am sorry, Beathan, but there is no time to rest. We should have hours of safety—the time it takes the Haunts to return to their masters and then cover the distance to us again—but we must cover more ground and build a lead on our pursuers. If we push hard, we may be able to make the port town of Wendall Harbor. It is perhaps a half day's journey from where we are now." Philip was again assuming control since he knew the lay of the land in this area, having spent time here off and on during his years as a Collector.

"Lead on then, mate. I've never been one to shirk an honest day's work," Beathan said jokingly through his tiredness.

"Really? Is that so? I never figured you for much of an advocate of honesty." Philip grasped Beathan's hand good-naturedly and hauled him to his feet.

"Our little secret." Beathan winked at his friend as the four of them wearily began to plod east in the lessening light of evening.

CHAPTER FIFTEEN

They ran through the waning light of late afternoon and into the dimness of twilight and then night. However, the wounded shuffling of their legs couldn't carry them much further. Philip felt like he would fall over if he tried to run another step.

"Alright, only Alayna is fit to run like this, and maybe you too, although I don't know exactly what your capabilities are." Philip directed the end of his statement towards Azir. He wasn't sure how much of the vampire's Elfas attributes were still present in him now, after transitioning into a hybrid.

"We do need a rest," Beathan agreed with him.

Alayna just nodded, looking less winded than any of them. Azir's dark eyes glinted in the starlight as he gazed at Philip, but he didn't say anything. He was keeping his secrets close about his capabilities.

"We'll set up camp here for a few hours of rest. We can't spend all night, but a few hours shouldn't ruin the lead we've built on the Haunts. Besides, it won't do any of us any good to collapse before we've reached Wendall Harbor."

Philip watched as Alayna sat down gracefully in the dirt where they had chosen to stop. She could make mud look like a palace. The salt water from their swim to shore had dried and left crusted patterns of white along the brown of her leggings. Stars speckled the sky above and a half-full moon shone brightly in the heavens, but nothing could compare to her. Philip was about to speak to her when Azir sat down next to Alayna and whispered something. Philip felt a surge of satisfaction as he saw Alayna shake her head and snub the vampire, leaning away from him. But then Philip watched as the vampire whispered something again and this time Alayna didn't pull away. This time she cocked her ear to listen.

Philip cleared his throat. "I'm going to do a quick check of our perimeter, make sure of the safety of our surroundings."

"I'll accompany ya', mate," Beathan rose on weary legs to walk with him into the darkness away from the camp.

The half-fairy turned knowing eyes on Philip as they secured the vicinity of their camp. "It may not be what it looks." He spoke seriously, with none of his usual fairy flippancy.

"What do you mean?" Philip pretended not to understand.

"Ya' don't have to play it that way with me, Mr. Collector. I know what's got ya' in a right twisted mess inside. An' I'm tellin' ya' it may not be what it looks like."

"Well, what it looks like is Alayna is growing awfully cozy with a bloodsucker!" Philip was surprised at his vehemence. Jealousy was one thing, but this anger felt like a slow burn boiling up all the frustration and fury inside of him. He was not a jealous man, or at least Alayna had never given him cause before.

"I'm just sayin', mate, don't go jumpin' t' conclusions." Beathan cautioned him, again showing more patience and restraint than his usual worry-free self.

"Azir must be using his vampire powers on her. A vampire can learn to make its vocal chords a weapon all their own—a siren song to its prey. I know he wants her, I can see the way he looks at her." Philip was venting now, ranting his worry and fear.

"Maybe so." The fairy paused, and then spoke on after a moment's thought. "But it may be somethin' slightly different. Don't go startin' a fight just now without proof."

Philip tilted his head quizzically. "What else could it mean?"

"I mean, that Azir contacted her mentally while he was in transition —in the midst of it. We have no bloody idea what the effects of that might've been." Beathan shrugged his shoulders and spread his hands as if not wanting to voice anything further—anything worse.

Philip took a moment to consider that thought. "There was a lot of pain in Norway when she received the mental contact." He spoke slowly, teasing the notion out as he vocalized it. "And at sea she mentioned that it felt like there was a residue of some kind left over from the mind to mind connection." Philip felt sick to his stomach wondering what might have happened, what that message might have resulted in.

Beathan stayed silent, likely feeling guilty that he had been the one to suggest that mental contact to Azir. Granted, he hadn't known the vampire was no longer purely one of the Elfas, but still, guilt could change the way a person viewed the past, and the accuracy of their choices and actions.

"Enough, Philip, we can do no more good by ponderin' and imaginin' the what ifs of the world."

Philip nodded. "Let's head back to camp."

They walked quietly back and as they approached they saw Alayna let out a reluctant but genuine chuckle at something the vampire had said. She smothered her laughter as they walked up and scooted herself just a few inches further away from the vampire than where she had previously been sitting. Not that there had been anything improper about their proximity—they had not been sitting closely enough to imply intimacy. Yet, Alayna avoided Philip's eyes for some reason, while Azir's piercingly black eyes held Philip's stare above his slightly smirking mouth. The vampire was pleased with himself.

"Having fun?" Philip asked as innocently as possible.

"Don't be like that, love," Alayna put a hand fondly on his arm as he sat next to her. "We were just talking."

"Like what?" Philip feigned a lack of understanding. Alayna just pursed her lips and looked at him the way she did whenever she thought he was being ridiculous. Well, maybe he was. First he exhibited jealous actions towards Captain Wake in Liverpool, and now this thing with Azir. Maybe Philip actually was a jealous man. It was a new way of viewing himself. Perhaps he had to work on containing those emotions. Maybe they were unnecessary.

You never need to worry, my love. Alayna voiced in his mind the way an Elfas could only do with someone with whom they shared great intimacy. Philip breathed out heavily and tried to forget his frustration and worries. He smiled at Alayna that everything was fine.

"Let's get some sleep. Just a few hours and then we have to move again. I'll take the first watch." Philip felt Alayna shift her weight as he spoke, seeking a more comfortable position while leaning against him.

"You sleep, Collector. These days I find the night... invigorating." Azir quirked a dark smile, but Philip could see through the fakery of his pleasant façade.

Philip decided not to answer the vampire and just ignored him. He closed his eyes and felt sleep begin to quickly wrap its inky tendrils around his tired mind.

———

PHILIP AWOKE to see Azir crouching near Alayna, lifting a lock of her hair and holding it with an oddly tender look on his face. Philip shifted and the vampire dropped the red-gold strands and stared at Philip with an intent gaze.

"We are connected, Collector. I did not plan it, but it happened. She and I share something you will never have." Azir whispered his words quietly enough that Alayna didn't awaken.

Philip didn't answer, but he felt his fears multiply. He desperately wished that the vampire was telling lies, but he had a feeling there was truth to the vampire's statement. The pain she had felt in Trondheim had been so different than any mental communication before, because the mental connection had been initiated by an Elfas transitioning into a vampire. What it meant for the future was uncertain. Would Azir be able to exert some sort of influence or mental control over Alayna because of the residue of his mind left on hers from their mental connection?

Philip shuddered at the thought. If there was one thing of which he was certain, it was that the half-vampire was utterly selfish. Philip hated the thought of a self-centered individual like him having some kind of control over the love of his life. What might he do to her? Would he drag her into a suicidal prison break? Philip's own mind began reminding him that he himself was far from the perfect mate. He shoved those thoughts away and woke Alayna so that he could stand up.

She stretched prettily and gave him a light kiss on the lips. "Time to go?"

"Yes, love," he replied.

"Perfect, it's been so long since I had a good run." Alayna smiled sleepily at her own joke. They had run nearly all day yesterday or least the parts of it when they hadn't been fighting and defending themselves.

They gathered what few belongings they had—a few weapons were about all there was—and set off again. They pushed forward steadily, pacing themselves. Philip believed they must have enough of a lead on their pursuers that they could afford not to sprint the entire way to Wendall Harbor.

After the passage of a few hours, Philip and Beathan began to breathe more heavily. Alayna and Azir looked like they were out for a morning stroll the way their lungs effortlessly powered their graceful bodies. They even seemed to run in unison with their legs moving at the exact same pace and rhythm.

No, you're imagining things! Philip scolded himself angrily. Jealousy was one thing, but he was beginning to grow paranoid about this perceived connection between Alayna and the vampire.

They stopped for a break near a stream corralled by two mossy banks. Philip collapsed by the water on the downy green moss and grass and cupped a few handfuls of water into his mouth greedily. He felt the tug of half-healed wounds as he moved. The pace they had set since leaving St. Thomas's had prevented his body from healing itself completely. The few hours of rest from last night had helped but it had not been enough. He felt slower, more sluggish than he should. He would just have to dig deep within himself and find some extra grit to draw upon.

"Let's rest for a few minutes here. The port town is not much farther down the coast, an hour or two's journey at most. So rest and drink up while you can." He finished by cupping another handful of water to his mouth.

"Thirsty are you?" Azir peered at Philip with his unnerving gaze. Philip had faced a lot of vampires in his day but something about this one was different. Perhaps it was the fact that he was a hybrid and the unknown capabilities that provided made Philip uneasy. He disliked not knowing his opponents' weak points. And there was no doubt in his mind that the vampire was his opponent. In more ways than one.

"We have been running." Philip answered levelly.

"Yes, exertion always does make me... thirsty," the vampire smiled showing his teeth, his delicate tongue curling up and over one fang and then onto his upper lip as he licked.

"Stop it, Azir," Alayna said with her usual exasperation—a tone she usually reserved for Philip.

"Whatever do you mean, Alayna?" The vampire asked innocently.

She just stared at the vampire with a reproachful face until Azir lifted his hands slightly in cordial surrender. It almost looked to Philip as if she had been speaking mentally—mind to mind—with the vampire. But that could only happen between people who were intimate in some way.

As if feeling Philip's eyes and guessing his line of thought Alayna cast an uncomfortable glance in his direction. When had Philip become the source of her discomfort? The question unsettled him greatly.

Philip stared at the vampire with a gaze like a knife. He felt the anger building within him. This vampire was testing his patience and good will to the extreme. Besides, Philip had not forgotten the attack by Azir in the cell, when he had drunk Philip's blood. Payback was bound to be due at some point.

Azir stared right back, a half smile on his face, that secretive look as if he knew something other people didn't. Then he turned back to Alayna.

"Alayna, my dear, have you ever seen Romania? It is a wonderful place. I traveled there some time ago before..." He didn't finish his sentence. "I think that I may like to return there and pay the land a long visit. Would you like to accompany me when I do?"

"I..." Alayna began to speak but Philip interrupted her.

"Listen up vampire, you are not one of us. You are not wanted. You're nothing more than a vile bloodsucker, a parasite to our escape." Philip felt Beathan's restraining hand on his shoulder as he had unwittingly taken an aggressive step towards the Azir.

"Vampire and nothing more? No, I think not. I am much more than that. Why do you think the sun does not burn me? And believe me, I am also much more than a casual acquaintance to your lovely Alayna." Azir looked at Alayna. "Aren't I, my dear?"

"Easy, Azir," Beathan said, "now's not the time t' go provokin' one another."

"Be quiet half-human," the vampire spat scornfully. "You are the worst type of hybrid."

"Shut up, vampire." Philip felt his anger mounting. Insulting his fairy friend, and insinuating who knew what between himself and Alayna, Azir was close to pushing Philip's normally level head into the rashness of rage. Philip could feel the wildness within him—his trollish belligerence —growing with each of the vampire's words.

"Azir, stop. Please." Alayna spoke a bit hesitantly.

Azir turned to Alayna and cupped her cheek, speaking only to her now. "Do not forget my sweet, I have been inside your head. I know you in a way he never will. I can give you things he never can. We are connected now, for always."

Philip felt sick seeing the lingering look being shared between them. Then Alayna blinked and shook her head slightly as if dazed.

"What are you doing to her!" Philip shouted. White-hot rage billowed inside of him like a fiery wind he had to expel in some way or another. He had to act. He coiled his muscles and then sprung forward tackling the vampire in a furious motion.

Azir snarled the way his kind did when in a fight. Philip felt fangs bite deeply into his shoulder as they collided with the ground in a heap of limbs. They rolled, each trying to gain the upper hand. Azir went for his throat hissing and growling like a predator sensing the kill.

But Philip tapped into his strength and swung a heavy callused fist into the vampire's face. He hit him again and again, and then head-butted him, leaving the vampire unconscious and listless in the dirt and moss. And just like that, it was over. It had been a short, brutal fight, but Philip's surprise attack had given him the upper hand. Vampires were exceedingly dangerous, but a brawler as strong as Philip had the upper hand when overtop of a vampire on the ground like he had been with Azir.

Philip stood and Alayna rushed to his side. "Are you alright, Philip?"

"Are you?" Philip asked right back, letting her check his bite wound.

Alayna averted her eyes and didn't answer. Philip tilted her chin upwards to look her in the eyes. "Alayna, talk to me. There is nothing to be ashamed of."

She sighed. "The residue I told you of while we were at sea, you remember?" Philip nodded his assent. "Well, it grew stronger in St. Thomas's. I followed the connection and found the cell. And the longer I am near Azir the stronger the residue feels. It's like..." She paused not wanting to voice her next thought.

Philip finished the thought for her. "It's like you're connected somehow."

Alayna nodded regretfully. "But it's not real, love. It's not how I really feel."

"What do you feel?"

"I admit, around Azir there is this... pull on my mind. A desire to look at him, speak to him. But as soon as I look at you that feeling fades like a dream in the night. When I look at you, Philip, I feel clear headed."

"So he's using his vampiric abilities to control your mind?" Philip asked trying to understand and trying not to feel jealous. He had to support Alayna right now through whatever it was that was happening to her.

"No."

"No?" Philip asked incredulously.

Alayna answered. "Well, at least I don't think so. To be fair, I don't think he really understands it either. I do not believe he made this happen intentionally. I think he feels a similar pull when he sees me."

"That may be, but he is dangerous, and whatever the root cause, he is trying to exploit this connection and persuade you to leave with him. You don't want to leave, do you?" Philip ended with a question that felt like it was ripping his guts out simply to ask it.

"Absolutely not! I love you, Philip. This mental connection is nothing more than a supernatural side effect. It's not special, not some version of twisted fate. It is something to be fixed." Alayna went into Philip's arms as she finished speaking and he held her close for a moment.

They came apart and Philip put a hand on the stake at his belt. "Well there is one way to solve this, to fix this problem." He glanced at the unconscious hybrid vampire on the ground.

Alayna paused and then cupped Philip's face in both her hands. "You are not a murderer. And for all his faults, I do not wish death upon Azir. At least not by your hand."

"Fine," Philip said sourly, acquiescing to her wishes. It would have been more pleasing than just about anything to drive a stake through that one's heart.

"Err... I hate t' interrupt such an important discussion, but there seems t' be a wee bit o' a problem." Beathan interjected, pulling their focus away from the vampire prostrate on the ground.

"What is it?" Philip asked.

Beathan pointed behind them. "Looks like I've come t' pay us another visit," the fairy said bleakly.

To the west, Philip watched as the other Beathan ran lightly towards them, its face blank and focused like an arrow seeking a target. Philip swore as he saw the three other Haunts enter his view right behind the first.

"What do we do?" Alayna asked.

"I don't know," Philip answered hopelessly. Nobody survived a fight with the Haunts.

CHAPTER SIXTEEN

"Can you shield us again?" Philip asked Beathan, although even if the fairy could do so, it wouldn't help the way it had last time. The last time they had only needed to last a few hours until the Deadbloods—the Haunts—had needed to return to their masters. However, this time, it was different. Judging by how quickly the Haunts had caught up with him and his companions, Philip guessed that the Blood Mages had met them somewhere on the road. The mages must not have awaited them at St. Thomas's, but rather had come to meet them partway. It accounted for the speed with which the Haunts had overtaken Philip's group. It also meant that outlasting the Haunts, this time behind a shield, was unlikely, because the mages were no doubt fairly close by and the Haunts would not need to give up and leave as quickly as the last time.

The small hope was dashed anyway, as Beathan shook his head doubtfully. "I do not know if I could make a big enough shield for all of us. I scarcely was able to withstand the pressure last time, and my body needs rest to recover, rest I've not had nearly enough of." Beathan tugged subconsciously at the bandages over his wrists. He'd been bled heavily in the prison.

"Could you shield one person? Or maybe... two?"

Beathan shrugged his shoulders in a non-committal way. "I can try, mate." The fairy's eyes were sad.

Alayna seemed to follow the direction of his thinking. "No! Absolutely not, Philip. I will not be sequestered away behind some invisible wall while you fight and die."

"There is no other choice, love. It's too dangerous. I couldn't bear it if you died because of me." Philip heard the pleading enter his voice. He didn't stop it. They had only moments before the danger was upon them and he needed Alayna to be safe.

Alayna stared at him bitterly. "Please. Please, Alayna. Do this for me. Under no circumstance are you to leave the protection of the barrier. Please." Philip was begging now.

Alayna grabbed a handful of his hair and kissed him fiercely. Then stepped beside Beathan. First, Philip heard the half-fairy mutter a concealment spell, flicking one of his jewels in the process, and Azir winked out of existence where he was lying a few feet from them. However, Philip was not surprised by the vampire's disappearance, he was accustomed to things vanishing around Beathan. Concealment spells were second nature to Beathan and were so easy as to require hardly any effort on his part. Philip could have done without the fairy's protection of the vampire.

Next, Beathan put an arm around Alayna, drew her close and then spoke the defensive charm, touching his new stone ring in the process. Philip put a hand forward and touched an invisible wall surrounding the two people about whom he cared the most in all the world. It was surprising to realize that somehow Beathan had managed to become such an important part of his world. Alayna made sense, but the fairy-gypsy was much more confounding. Well, love and affection didn't always make sense Philip supposed, as he turned his back on the ones he cared about and prepared to meet his fate.

He just had to kill them. He didn't have to survive this fight himself. If he could just prevent them from taking Alayna that would be enough. 'Just', he laughed out loud at the ludicrous nature of thinking that killing four Haunts was anything less than grandiose in nature.

Philip set his feet and drew the sword he had taken off the dead guard. He had no doubt that at some point this fight would come down to his worn knuckles and callused fists, but for now he would take any advantage he could get. The sword was long and sharp, well cared for by its previous owner. Perhaps he could inflict a wound or two with it.

The other Beathan led the way followed by the other Alayna, Azir, and bringing up the rear was the replica of Philip, himself. What was the strategy here? The Haunts formed some kind of psychic connection with their targets. That meant that although the other version of himself wouldn't possess the same strength and healing ability as he did, it would nonetheless have imported much of the training and battle tactics from Philip's mind into its own.

That meant the other Philip would be dangerous. The replica Alayna would likely be the least dangerous. Alayna was smart and a quick thinker, but she was not combat trained like Philip. The other Azir wouldn't have all the vampire's traits but it would likely have imported the predatory instinct through its psychic connection with the incapacitated Azir. It would do so because the predatory instinct was primarily a mental, internal gifting. That made the other Azir dangerous. However, something told Philip that the biggest challenge would be the replica Beathan. The half-fairy was clever. Philip had the sense that he didn't know the half of just how crafty and wily the hybrid gypsy was. That intelligence and strategic thinking would belong to the other Beathan now. Philip had fought the real Beathan once, months ago back in New York. He had been hard pressed then to contain the fairy. This replica Beathan would not have the speed or agility of the fairy, but the Haunts could wink in and out of substantial form. That gift more than tipped the advantages in their favor.

Philip sorted and filed away these thoughts quickly, the way a combat trained soldier was taught to do and readied himself for the fight. The four Haunts arrayed themselves around him in a square of sorts, then into a triangle as one of the Haunts—the other Alayna—broke off and began to test the invisible barrier that was magically erected by Beathan. Philip saw perspiration break out on the fairy's face as he resisted the attempts by the other Alayna to penetrate the barrier. That was his fight. Philip had to focus on his own dire situation.

The other Philip, Beathan, and Azir circled Philip casually yet with purpose, the way a pack of predators circle prey they know to be dead soon. It was not a comforting realization to see that the Haunts viewed him as already beaten.

They engaged with speed. The replica vampire rushed Philip and Philip swung his sword in a lighting quick horizontal sweep that would have cleaved the creature in two if it hadn't disappeared just before the blade touched it. Philip turned to look over his shoulder as the replica vampire materialized out of thin air right behind him. Philip had no time to register the shock of seeing what he had known would happen, as the other two attacked. The other Philip struck a blow to his side, not particularly forceful, but perfectly placed to open up one of his wounds from Liverpool. Philip felt the blood flow. The other Philip's psychic link to his own mind would give it a glimpse into his weaknesses, including, injured points.

The other Beathan flashed in close and struck a flurry of blows to Philip's face and torso and Philip blocked the blows as best he could and absorbed the others. He swung a mighty fist towards the replica fairy but connected with only air as the other Beathan dematerialized and then materialized back into physical form a few feet away.

Philip shifted his focus to the replica vampire who was now attacking again from behind. Whipping his sword around with pace and precision, he managed to knick the creature's shoulder before it would wink out and then back into form in another place. The wound he'd inflicted on the creature wasn't grave, but Philip felt a small sense of satisfaction, watching blood seep from the wound on its shoulder. It stared malevolently at Philip, with the first true emotions he had seen on any of the Haunts' faces since the creatures had arrived.

The three Haunts didn't talk. Their silence was echoed by the silence of Alayna and Beathan behind the barrier. What was there to say? They watched him fight a losing battle, while the other Alayna tested and tested again Beathan's mental and physical fortitude.

Philip gritted his teeth and fought. He fought harder than he'd ever fought before. Slash and cut with his sword, swing of a fist. Most of the time he caught nothing but air, but once more he was fortunate enough to slice a shallow wound on one of the beast's—the other Philip's—thigh, slowing it slightly. He also landed a punch into the face of the other Beathan, the impact of which sounded with a satisfying thud.

However, by and large, the three of them made a meal of Philip. His sword was snatched out of his hand. Blows rained down upon him from sudden attacks out of previously thin air. The power to dematerialize and then reappear at will was a powerful one indeed. Philip didn't know what he could do to stave off the inevitable.

It was time to gamble.

An attack came from the replica Beathan and as it winked out of existence, Philip anticipated, guessing it would do so and then shifting his stance to be ready for where he thought it might reappear. Surprisingly—perhaps fortunately—the replica fairy reappeared right where Philip had guessed it would be. Philip grabbed the replica fairy by the head and twisted, wrenching the neck at a grotesque angle. Astonishment registered on the creature's face right before it died. Lucky indeed, Philip thought. And amusingly, in the midst of the chaos and confusion of the fight he found a moment of laughter realizing he had outwitted the fairy. Even though it wasn't the real Beathan, there was still a sense of pleasure in knowing that he'd outsmarted some version of the insufferable half-breed.

Two on one now. The other Azir and the other Philip circled in close and attacked in tandem. The other Azir might not have all the physical powers of a real vampire but it did have the appearance—meaning it had fangs that could tear. Not for the first time that day, Philip felt the ripping of his flesh as vampire teeth penetrated his skin. The other Philip slithered in close and struck a stunningly direct blow to the wound he'd sustained fighting the Minotaur. He gasped at the pain, just as the teeth of the other Azir clamped into the flesh of his neck. Philip tapped into his strength and flung the replica vampire off of him towards a tree. Right as the other Azir looked like it would collide with the tree with breathtaking impact, it winked out of existence and reappeared a few feet from Philip. The two Haunts again began circling Philip.

Philip knew that he had to fight better or he and his companions had no hope of survival. He'd killed one Haunt with more than some luck. But he needed to kill the rest. Philip released his inner monster. He let the troll blood within him sing. He let the rush of the fight set his veins on fire with delight and anticipation. Tapped into the strength and power of his blood.

He then married this wildness with his tactical, combat training. He was a skilled soldier, a trained fighter. A former Collector. He was a supernaturally strong being with the battle training of a professional warrior. Philip melded those two sides of himself. If he was going to die here, he was going to go out with everything he had. He would leave no doubt in anyone's mind that he was a foe with which to be reckoned.

He anticipated. He remembered his battle training. Know your opponent. The other Philip would be more cautious, its psychic link with himself would ensure that similarity. It would be the more measured fighter. The other vampire would feel the same hate for him that its psychically connected prey—Azir—did. That meant it was likely to be the more aggressive. Philip pulled a knife in his right hand and a stake in the left. He feinted one way then the other. He stepped towards the replica Philip turning away from the other Azir. Now! He thought. The other vampire would attack his back now. Philip spun and swung with the power and might of his blood, he struck with the efficiency of his training. Sure enough, the other vampire was leaping towards his exposed back and it skewered itself on Philip's stake just as he had anticipated it would. He pulled the stake free and struck again before the injured Haunt could dematerialize. Dead. Two gone.

Philip faced the other version of himself. This would be a challenge. They leaped at each other and began the desperate battle. The creature's power to wink in and out of physical form gave it a definite advantage, making Philip pay for his mistakes and for his lessening speed as his injuries mounted and old wounds broke fresh. Yet, Philip fought as never before. He used his powers and his mind, his training, and anticipation.

Almost as often as he was struck and injured, he in turn delivered blows. He saw the other Philip shake its head groggily as he landed a particularly vicious punch to its face. He opened a cut on its chest with his knife. But in turn, he felt himself weaken. The Haunt winked in and out, appearing just in time to strike the various wounds on Philip's body, courtesy of its psychic link telling it of his injuries. It inflicted new wounds. Philip felt his face swell from a particularly hard blow to the head. They battled for what seemed like hours. Philip couldn't shake the surreal feeling of being pitted against himself. A nightmare from which he couldn't wake.

The Haunt blinked out of existence like a lightning bug at night, then back to form just to Philip's left. It grabbed his arm and struck with both fists, the torque snapping Philip's bone. He screamed. But in the midst of the pain he guessed. He appraised his opponent. It was him. Another version of him. A smart fighter. Having just struck a crippling blow it would step back, regroup, and attack again at the right moment. It winked out of existence and Philip lunged forward to where he hoped the Haunt would reappear.

It materialized back into existence right in front of him. With his good hand, Philip swiftly reached forward and grasped its throat. He squeezed. There was popping and crunching. Philip's troll-infused might coupled with the adrenalin and desperation of the fight gave him the strength to crush the Haunt's windpipe. He dropped it to the ground, watching dispassionately as the other version of himself choked to death.

He turned towards Alayna and Beathan only to realize that he had forgotten there was still one Haunt left. The other Alayna stared at him blankly. It had had no success in breaching Beathan's barrier. It stepped away from the invisible wall towards him. Apparently it would settle for Philip.

He was exhausted, wounded in too many places, with a shattered arm on top of everything. Desperation tinged his thoughts and he charged rashly towards the other Alayna. It felt queer trying to kill anything that resembled the one he loved. The replica Elfas dematerialized and he stumbled to his knees in front of the barrier. His eyes met Alayna's tiredly for a moment and then he stood and turned to face the last remaining Haunt.

It was clear he was in no condition to fight. The other Alayna might have been the least dangerous of the four, but it had caught him at the right moment. He swung a ragged blow at the creature and missed. The Haunt didn't even have to use its power to avoid his swing, it just stepped aside agilely. Pain from the shattered arm and the other wounds he bore threatened to engulf Philip's mind. He stumbled forward again to engage in a last attempt to end this. One more, he thought. One more and they can escape, they can go free. He lunged toward the other Alayna and she dodged easily, felling him with a high kick to the temple.

As he lay on the ground trying to regroup, attempting to rise through the blinding pain, he saw the other Alayna pick up the knife that Philip had dropped when his arm had broken. The replica Alayna knelt over him and raised the knife, eyes focused on Philip, its prey. Just as the blade was about to fall, another knife flew through the air and into the chest of the Haunt.

The Haunt looked in stunned disbelief at the blade protruding from its body and then toppled over. The real Alayna strode forward and pulled the knife out of the body and then quickly slashed the throat of her replica just to be sure of its death.

"Aren't you glad I didn't listen?" Alayna looked at him pointedly.

Philip could only muster a weak grin. "Yes, I am."

"Quite a fight, mate. Remind me not to cross ya'." Beathan helped him to his feet, as Philip clutched his wounded arm to his side. "I thought ya' said the beasties couldn't be beaten?"

"There is a first time for everything, I suppose." Philip answered somewhat wonderingly himself. He really didn't know how he had survived. Only by combining his wild nature with the keen instincts groomed in him during his years as a Collector could he have succeeded. It had been skill that had won today, but luck also. Philip couldn't help but feel like it was a miracle he was still alive.

"What now?" Beathan asked.

"We move on," Philip said tiredly. "Wendall Harbor cannot be more than an hour or two from here. Hopefully, our luck will hold and there will be a ship in the small port that is ready to depart."

"After we tend to your wounds." Alayna said firmly, already doing her best to patch him up. Philip nodded in acquiescence. He needed the tending. Alayna bound him up as best as possible and fit his arm into a sling of sorts. It was all they could do for now.

"What about him?" Beathan inclined his head toward the still unconscious vampire.

Philip walked over and kicked him. It felt good to do so for some reason. The vampire stayed unconscious. "I didn't think I hit him that hard."

"He's not dead, I can tell." Alayna volunteered, then looked a bit self-conscious for doing so. She was clearly still not sure how Philip would react to her saying such things. To be fair, Philip wasn't sure either. It would be a careful dance between the two of them for now in regards to the subject of her connection to the hybrid.

"Well, we are in no shape to carry him. Besides, I could do without his company. Maybe he was weaker than we thought from not having consumed enough blood. Perhaps with time he'll heal." Philip scratched his head with his good hand as he thought and spoke.

"I'll bind a lasting concealment spell t' him. Should last a few hours. Hopefully he'll awaken by then and make his own way from there." The fairy walked over to the vampire and kneeled down, muttering some kind of incantation.

Or hopefully he won't, Philip thought sourly. The world wouldn't be a worse place without the vampire.

They set off at a hobbled walk and covered the distance to the port in less time than Philip had expected. The distance was short, and even in their weakened state they were soon walking into the small port town and making their way towards the harbor.

A ship, again, was what they needed.

CHAPTER SEVENTEEN

The three of them stood shoulder to shoulder in the bow of the ship, away from inquisitive ears. They had been lucky. A ship bound for London had been departing within the hour and they had secured passage. The sea air was misty with fog as the sun from earlier disappeared. Tendrils of gray cloud streaked through the ship weaving their way between people and masts.

This weather was common for the English coast, and Philip had experienced it for years. It reminded him of his childhood. This ship was bound for London and from there they could make a connection and secure passage to nearly anywhere they liked. Philip was still pondering where they should go. Only one thing was certain—they had to go somewhere fast, and likely far from here. Or at least he did. His blood spilled during the breakout from St. Thomas's ensured that.

"What are you thinking about, Philip?" Alayna asked, leaning closer to him against the damp cold front rolling in.

"The past, the future, and what comes next."

"An' what does come next, mate?" Beathan inquired.

This was the part Philip had hoped to avoid, at least for a few more hours of peace. But the question hung in the air, waiting to be answered.

"Philip?" Alayna prodded him softly.

Philip sighed. "I have to go—far. I have to run and never look back."

"What are you talking about, Philip?" Alayna's voice was tinged with worry now. She didn't know. Neither of Philip's companions knew the price he had paid to free his friend. He had risked more than his life to set Beathan free. He had wagered a lifetime of pursuit against his fairy friend's escape and loss. Oh, he had freed Beathan, but he had paid in blood and that blood was what would betray him.

"What have ya' done, my friend?" All joking was gone from Beathan's voice. "What did ya' do for me?"

There was nothing for it but to explain. "The Blood Mages do more than just control the Deadbloods who guard St. Thomas's. They can track people by their blood, like a magical tracing spell. But they can only do so with creatures or people from whom they have already gained a blood sample." Philip watched the confusion grow on his friends' faces.

"What do you mean by that?" Alayna questioned.

"I mean you both are free to go. You could sail wherever you wish and likely never be found. Or least not tracked by the Guild by your blood. I, on the other hand, do not have that luxury. All Collectors are required to give a blood sample to the Blood Mages at St. Thomas's upon entry to our profession. The Blood Mages spell the blood sample, and can use it to locate the owner—the Collector—of the sample. It is a safeguard against betrayal.

"Long ago, the Guild realized that the only weakness to their prison at St. Thomas's was a danger from the inside—from within the Guild itself. A mutiny could result in the release of dangerous captive creatures. Loyalty runs strong within the Guild's organization, but even they were aware that circumstances can sometimes arise that cause a person to go against their history of compliance." Philip gestured to himself as an example.

"So, these magicians have a blood sample o' yours, eh?"

Philip nodded to his fairy friend. "Yes. I gave it willingly, never thinking that I would betray the Guild. However, I was wounded. My blood loss within the walls of St. Thomas's during our escape left a clue as to who engineered the escape. They will test the blood residues from the battle. They will match it with my blood sample and activate the tracking spell. It is a difficult and lengthy spell, which is why they never did it before when they thought me dead from the events of last winter in New York. Why waste the energy of their most prized servants, the Blood Mages, on a dead man? Yet, they will now realize that I am alive and a traitor. They will activate the spell on my blood that allows them to trace my blood and follow my location wherever I go."

Beathan smiled a wry, sad smile. "Haven't ya' ever heard that the price o' consortin' with a fairy is high. Too high to pay?" He shook his head and placed a hand on Philip's shoulder. "Ya' knew this was likely to occur, an' yet ya' still came to me aid. In some ways, I wish ya' hadn't, knowing this now."

"You two could still leave. We could part ways and they would only follow me." Philip proposed the idea to the two of them. Part of him had never expected Beathan to stay with him after this anyway. The fairy went where he wanted, when he wanted. He lived of his own accord. Alayna was a different matter.

He turned to gauge Alayna's reaction to his proposal.

"You're an idiot if you think I am leaving you," was all she said. It was enough of an answer for him. He turned and faced out over the water. From London they could go anywhere.

A quizzical thought occurred to him. Here Philip was about to be chased for the rest of his life and he had never received an answer from Beathan as to how the fairy had been captured. It must have been a funny story. He deserved an answer, and so he asked the fairy what had happened.

Beathan responded. "Was watching a fawn bewitch a lord out o' his life's savings an' it was a mite too comical t' ignore. I got careless an' they nabbed me."

"That's it?" Philip had expected something more grandiose.

"That's it."

They stood in silence again for a while watching the ocean and the grey horizon. Alayna clasped hands with Philip. It was a comfort to feel her hand in his.

"So, after London, where are you headed?" Beathan asked Philip after a time.

Philip looked at Alayna and she shrugged. *You decide.* Her voice echoed in his mind.

"I don't know. East, or maybe south." Philip responded.

"Well?" Beathan asked.

"Well, what?"

"Which is it?"

"East." Philip said calmly.

"What do ya' know, I believe I'm headed in the same direction." The fairy kept a straight face, but there was a betraying twinkle in his eye.

Philip shook his head and laughed softly. "And if I had said south?"

"Then I would've been heading south."

"We'll be hunted," Philip cautioned, all mirth gone.

"I've been hunted before," Beathan said indifferently.

The expanse of horizon stretching before them was as murky with fog and mist as their future was clouded with uncertainty. What was to come should be terrifying, or worrisome at least. Yet, instead Philip felt content.

The three of them stood shoulder to shoulder leaning against the rail, ready to face whatever lay ahead.

Keep reading for a preview of
The Collector #2
Blood Loss

THANK YOU FOR READING

Did you enjoy this book?

We invite you to leave a review at the website of your choice, such as Goodreads, Amazon, Barnes & Noble, etc.

DID YOU KNOW THAT LEAVING A REVIEW...

- Helps other readers find books they may enjoy.
- Gives you a chance to let your voice be heard.
- Gives authors recognition for their hard work.
- Doesn't have to be long. A sentence or two about why you liked the book will do.

Don't miss out on your next favorite book!

Join the Melange Books mailing list at
www.melange-books.com/mail.html

Subscriber Perks Include:

- First peeks at upcoming releases.
- Exclusive giveaways.
- News of book sales and freebies right in your inbox.
- And more!

ABOUT THE AUTHOR

Mathias Colwell grew up in far Northern California exploring redwood forests and cloudy beaches. He loves God, his family, and friends. Mathias has been a writer for most of his life, drafting his first stories as young as eight years of age. His desire to write fantasy was inspired by such authors as J.R.R. Tolkien, David Eddings and the late Robert Jordan. He is an avid traveler and all-around adventurer, having visited or lived in 27 countries. His travels have led him around the world to five continents including stays in Siberia, Spain, and Chile, and he attributes many of his passions and goals in life to these experiences. In his free time, he enjoys reading, outdoor activities such as soccer, snowboarding and water sports. Mathias has a passion for issues pertaining to social justice and human rights and hopes to influence these areas in the future.

twitter.com/MathiasColwell
facebook.com/Mathias-GB-Colwell-225647397579547

ALSO BY MATHIAS G. B. COLWELL

with Melange Books

The Collector Series
The Collector

Blood Loss

Menagerie of Shadow

Dark Arrow Trilogy
Dusk Runner

Entrance to Dark Harbor

Black Water Well (coming soon!)

Novellas
An Age of Mist

A Burning Hope

www.ingramcontent.com/pod-product-compliance
Lightning Source LLC
Chambersburg PA
CBHW020137180626
46810CB00004B/1607